LOVER IN LINGERIE

LINGERIE #15

PENELOPE SKY

Hartwick Publishing

Lover in Lingerie

Copyright © 2018 by Penelope Sky

All rights reserved.

CONTENTS

1

BONES

VANESSA'S pregnant belly had gotten so big that it limited our positions during lovemaking. She was almost finished with her seventh month, and her distended stomach became rounder and rounder. My son was going to be a big boy, judging by the way he constantly needed more room in her tiny body.

Now I liked to stand at the side of the bed with her ass hanging over the edge. I cradled her legs in my arms and thrust inside her, careful not to hit her stomach. She was getting uncomfortable in her pregnancy, her back and feet hurting, so I did all the work.

Not that I minded.

She held on to my wrists as I gently thrust inside her, moving my big dick through her tightness. Despite her dull aches and pains, she was still just as aroused by me as ever.

I watched her come for me, finding pleasure for a moment before she returned to her constant discomfort.

She dug her nails into my skin and whispered my name over and over, full of my cock, my baby, and my love.

I came as she ended, filling her pussy with my seed. I didn't know how I would feel about her pregnancy before she became pregnant, but now I knew it was another thing that turned me on. Seeing that belly every day got me aroused in a way nothing else ever had. I loved watching her waddle around the house, my son growing stronger inside her every day. When he was born, it would be time for me to be a father. But until that moment, I was just a husband obsessed with my knocked-up wife.

I pulled out of her then kissed her belly, smothering every curve with my lips. She was as petite as she ever was, making her belly look even bigger. I trailed my lips up her body then kissed her mouth. "I love you, baby."

She ran her hands up my chest. "I love you too, husband."

I kissed the corner of her mouth before I pulled away. It was nighttime, and all the lights were off in the house. After Bosco stopped by last week, I was a little more paranoid than I had been before, but he hadn't shown up again. He didn't seem to be a threat, but now that I had a pregnant wife, even a hint of a threat was too much for me.

I went downstairs and checked on the rest of the

house one more time, including the infrared cameras that filmed throughout the night, before I came back to bed.

Vanessa was under the sheets with her head against the pillow. "Everything alright?"

"Yes." I got into bed beside her, still slightly uneasy about Bosco's visit. Just when I thought all our troubles were gone, Carmen had to sleep with the devil.

Vanessa picked up on my tension. She turned over and faced me, her hand over her stomach. "What is it?"

I never lied to her, so I chose to be silent.

"Griffin?"

"Go to bed, baby." My palm moved to her stomach, my fingers reaching out and covering most of her belly. He wasn't kicking right now, but I could still feel the life inside her, the life we made together.

She gave me that sassy look that told me she wasn't gonna drop this. "You've been weird all week. I've waited for you to tell me yourself, but you obviously are never gonna fess up."

I looked into her green eyes, the eyes that brought me comfort during my darkest times. I'd never told her about Bosco and the conversation we had outside. I didn't want to scare her. But since we both knew what Carmen was doing, it seemed strange to keep it a secret. "I know about Bosco."

Her eyes immediately lost their hostility. She tensed in a new way, her stomach even shifting slightly.

"I noticed her shop was closed one day, so I went to

her apartment. It was obvious she hadn't been there in months. Her mail hadn't been checked either. I spotted her car on his property, and that's when I knew."

All she did was sigh in response.

"Bosco and I talked about it." I skipped the part where he came to the house, but I didn't actually lie about it. "He told me about their arrangement, but he also made it clear he would let her go at the end. He threatened to hurt all of us if I said anything, so I agreed to be silent. Since their relationship is gonna end, I didn't see the point in fighting it. As long as Carmen isn't a prisoner, I suppose there's no real harm. I confronted Carmen about it and told her how disappointed I was. She assured me she would leave him when their arrangement was finished, understanding her family would never accept him. He isn't husband material, and he can't give her the life she wants."

Vanessa stayed quiet, absorbing all the information I'd just given her.

I watched every little reaction she made, wondering what she would say next.

She didn't deny that she already knew all of that. "I warned her it was a bad idea. She said she's looking for a relationship like ours, a man she can settle down with. She wants passion, devotion, and a man who can protect her. I told her he didn't fit the bill, that he was too dangerous and controlling. She agreed with me and tried to break things off. He refused, roping her into this three-month agreement."

I clenched my jaw. "Any man who has to force a woman to stay is no man at all."

She raised an eyebrow. "You're joking, right?"

I remembered the beginning of our relationship and her time as my prisoner. "Not the same. I was a different man then."

"At first, there was no deadline. He just wanted to keep her forever. But she negotiated to three months. He signed a contract and assured her he would let her go. She wanted an excuse to stay but also a way to leave —so she got what she wanted."

"I can't believe she actually likes this guy…"

"After what happened in the alleyway, I don't blame her. Now that she's with a powerful man, she feels safe."

"She would be safe if she didn't make stupid decisions," I snapped. "I offered to take her home, but she refused."

She placed her hand on my arm to calm me. "Griffin, she told me he's more than just the criminal mastermind of the underworld, that he's sweet, gentle, and kind."

I rolled my eyes.

"You understand you're being a huge hypocrite, right?"

"My personal life and my occupation were distinctly separate. I didn't bring work home with me. When it mattered, I walked away from that life and settled down with you. Now I have honest work and a simple life. Bosco is the job. He's constantly swarmed by the criminal plague. There's no separation. He's obsessed with money and violence. It's completely different."

"I think you're being unfair. He runs a casino. It's not like he was a hitman."

My wife was driving me nuts right now. "Are you saying you want Carmen to date this thug?"

"No, I—"

"Because it sounds like you're defending him."

Her eyes radiated rage. "Don't interrupt me."

I didn't dare do it again.

"I just think you're overreacting. The man said he would let her go if she wanted to leave. That means she's not a prisoner. She's there at her own discretion. I hated you when I first met you, but I started to see all of your good qualities."

"I didn't have good qualities. You just made me acquire them."

"Fine. Maybe the same thing is happening with Carmen. Maybe Bosco is changing for her."

I shook my head slightly.

"The relationship is gonna end soon, so it doesn't matter."

"It better end. But more importantly, it shouldn't have started in the first place." I gave her a look full of accusation. "You should have told me the second you knew about this."

"Excuse me?" She sat up, letting the sheet fall down to reveal her swollen tits. "She asked me not to. I would never betray her."

"Even though she was in danger?"

"That's not how she described it."

"You still should have told me. I could have handled it."

"Griffin," she said coldly. "I would never betray Carmen's trust. She made me promise not to say anything. I will never break a promise. If she were in any real danger, of course, I would have said something, but she never was."

I shook my head, still annoyed with her. "We could have stopped this a long time ago…"

"Griffin, Carmen is twenty-five. She owns her own business and has been on her own for six years now. She can do whatever she wants. She doesn't need us to boss her around and intervene."

"Again, this isn't some petty criminal that sells weed on the corner. This man is the most powerful guy in Florence."

"And she can hold her own pretty damn well. If not, she wouldn't tell me she felt safe with him. She would tell me she was afraid of him. That's not how she feels, Griffin. You need to let this go."

I loved Carmen like my own sister. She was the only one who'd treated me with respect when I tried to win over the Barsettis. She defended me and didn't treat me like some kind of psychopath. She knew I loved Vanessa —and gave me a real chance. "I love her very much. She's an amazing woman and deserves an amazing man."

Vanessa's eyes softened as she listened to me.

"I have a special place in my heart for her. She was kind to me when no one else was. She believed in us when no one else did. She never doubted my love for you, never doubted that my love was enough to overcome my flaws. I just want the best for her… I would die for her."

Vanessa's hand moved to mine, and she gently stroked her fingers over my knuckles. "I know, Griffin. That's why you need to trust her, to trust her instincts. She's a smart woman. She believed in you, and now you need to believe in her."

That was easier said than done. The Barsettis had become my family, and now I cared about all of them. I would lay down my life for any of them.

"Let's not worry until we actually have something to worry about." She rubbed my arm then kissed my shoulder. "You aren't going to tell my father and uncle, right?"

That was the worst part, keeping it from them. I worked with them every single day, had become a son to both of them. "What's gonna happen when they find out I knew the whole time?"

"They aren't gonna find out."

"And if they do?"

She sighed. "Carmen made you promise."

"That's not gonna be good enough, and you know it."

"Tell them you would have intervened if she was in real danger, but she obviously wasn't."

I still felt like shit for keeping this from the two men I respected most. "If they ask me point-blank, I can't lie. I'll never lie, and if that happens, then so be it."

"Why would they ask you that?"

"If they ask me if I know if Carmen's dating someone, I'll have to tell them."

"They aren't going to ask you that."

Probably not. But it was possible. "They might."

"Well, cross that bridge when you come to it. But I suspect you never will."

2

CARMEN

I WAS at the shop when Vanessa texted me.

Let's get lunch. We need to talk.

There was no doubt in my mind that Griffin and Vanessa had officially shared everything. I couldn't ignore her, so I agreed. *Alright. See you soon.* I locked up the shop then met her at our favorite place, a little bistro that had the best ravioli ever made.

Vanessa was already sitting when I walked inside, her chair farther away from the table to accommodate her round stomach. She didn't get up to hug me, and the horrified look on her face told me she noticed the black eye. "If that fucking piece of shit—"

"Wasn't him." I glanced around at the other tables, seeing the concerned looks on everyone's faces as they listened to a pregnant woman scream her head off. I fell into the chair across from her, embarrassed the thought even crossed her mind. "Chill."

"Then what happened? Your eyes are practically swollen shut, Carmen. If Griffin sees that, he's gonna hunt down Bosco with a knife."

"And that would be a mistake because it wasn't him. Bosco would never hurt me." Emotion entered my voice because I shouldn't even have to say that. Bosco put his life on the line to protect me. He wasn't afraid to make any sacrifice when it came to me.

"Then who did it?"

"I was in line at the bank when it got robbed."

"Oh my god. I saw that in the paper. You were there?"

I nodded. "Some guy tried to take the necklace my father got me, so I fought him. He punched me in the face, and then Bosco and his men came in. Bosco stabbed him to death and took care of the other men. If it weren't for Bosco and his security team, I would be dead right now." I had to set the record straight because Bosco wasn't the villain. He was the hero.

"Jesus, are you okay, Carmen?"

"I'm fine. It's a little painful, but the swelling has gone down."

"I'm so sorry." She placed her hand on mine. "That must have been terrifying."

"Not as terrifying as what happened in the alleyway. I knew Bosco was coming for me, so I was calm."

"Yeah…good thing he was there." She said the words with only partial sincerity.

"So you and Griffin finally talked about it."

She pulled her hand away and nodded. "Yes. He's not happy about it, Carmen."

"I know."

"And he cares about you so much. He says you're his favorite Barsetti and wants to make sure you have what you deserve. His heart is in the right place. I know he comes off as a caveman sometimes…but he adores you."

I already knew that. "He's a good man."

"He said he'll stay quiet about it. But he won't lie, so if our fathers come right out and ask him about it, he'll tell the truth."

His commitment to transparency was annoying. "Pain in the ass…"

"I know he is," she said with a slight smile. "He's willing to keep your secret, but he's not willing to sacrifice his reputation to do it. You've put him in a difficult position because he sees your father every day. If they ever find out about this and discover that Griffin knew…there will be trouble."

"Why does our family need to be so involved in every aspect of our lives?" I asked incredulously. "Other families aren't like this."

"Because other families don't care, which isn't a good thing. And if you dated a normal guy, then this would be a different situation. Then it wouldn't matter how long you kept it a secret because it really would be none of our business. But you probably wouldn't have kept it a secret this long because there would be no reason not to introduce him to your family."

"My father never actually said this to me, but he doesn't want to meet a man unless he's gonna be my husband. It was implied. So it would be too soon for that anyway." A part of me wished my personal life weren't so fascinating to everyone, but I also knew Vanessa was right. Everyone just wanted the best for me, and that meant I needed to be with the best guy.

"I get that," Vanessa said with a nod. "But since there're only a few weeks left, it doesn't matter. When you find the next guy, make sure he's not a crime lord, and everything should be just fine."

My expression immediately wilted at the thought of meeting someone new, dating someone new, sleeping with someone new… I couldn't picture a face different from Bosco's. I loved the strong lines of his jaw, the beauty of his bright eyes, and the hard muscles of his trim physique. I loved how tough he was, the way he commanded an entire room just by walking into it. And I loved how soft he was when it was just the two of us, when he was treating me like a delicate woman who needed affection.

Vanessa caught the look. "Griffin is under the impression this is gonna end in three weeks…I hope that's still the case."

I kept telling myself that's what was gonna happen, but now I didn't know anymore. Bosco was convinced I would never leave his side, not when we crossed the line and told each other that meaningful phrase. "I need to tell you something. You can't tell Griffin."

She covered her face with her palms before she dragged them down her cheeks. "Carmen, don't do this to me. I don't want to keep anything from my husband. It's too weird. We're honest with each other about everything."

"I'm sorry. But you're the person I confide every-thing to…"

She squinted her eyes like that was painful to hear. "Alright. What is it?"

I told her about The Butcher and the ring. I told her about the night Bosco fought him to the death.

Vanessa looked horrified. "They jumped in the ring together and fought like animals?"

"Yeah…"

"Jesus, that doesn't scare you?"

"No…it turned me on, honestly." Seeing Bosco fight like a carnal creature and claim his territory only made me respect him more. He turned into a primal man who only understood love and violence. "He's so power-ful, even without his suit and his men. His authority comes from who he is…not just his wealth. He didn't have to do that, but since I'm his woman, he wanted to. He wanted to break that man's bones and make him pay for what he did…while I watched. It was the manliest thing I'd ever seen."

Vanessa watched me, a wealth of emotions on her face. "Reminds me of something Griffin would do."

"Exactly."

"That man is hung up on you, Carmen. Why would he risk everything for you unless you were the most important person in his life?"

That was my opportunity to tell her my next batch of news. "Ruby called him one night. I got jealous, so I snatched the phone and talked to her…told her off for trying to take Bosco away from me."

"Good. Skank needs to know the boundaries."

"When I hung up, Bosco and I talked about it. I told him I was surprised he didn't go for it with her. He was a little offended by that. Then he told me he loved me. Said he didn't want anyone else, not when I'm the only woman he loves."

Vanessa didn't seem even slightly surprised by that. "And you told him the same thing."

"Well, no. I told him we were going our separate ways in three weeks, so I refused to say it back. But then he rescued me at the bank, and…I couldn't keep it inside any longer. I told him how I felt…and meant every single word."

Vanessa sighed before she ran her fingers through her hair. "This is bad. Griffin thinks it's gonna end."

"That's still my objective."

Vanessa cocked her head to the side and gave me an incredulous look, like what I'd just said was absolutely preposterous. "You love this man, and you're really going to leave him? I don't believe that, and I don't see how you can believe that. When I told

Griffin I loved him, there was no going back. We were in it together—for better or worse. There's power in those words. It'll bind you together for the rest of your life."

"He said I won't leave when the time comes…"

"Because he's not stupid. He's got you wrapped around his finger."

"And he's wrapped around mine." I knew I could ask Bosco for anything, and he would give it to me. "I made him promise he would never hurt any member of my family. I also made him promise not to threaten them either. He agreed…and even apologized for doing it in the past."

"Then what's next?" Vanessa asked. "The only thing to do is come clean about it."

"I don't see why I have to. I've only been with him for a few months. If I don't want to introduce him to my family, I don't have to. I'm not in danger, and I'm free to come and go as I please."

"Very true," Vanessa said. "But, secrets never stay secrets. I'm a testament to that. Even if Griffin and I stay quiet, you'll get caught somehow. Your father will stop by your apartment and realize you're never there. Your mom will see another text message on your phone, and that will incriminate you. You'll get caught in one of your lies. Something will catch up to you…it's only a matter of time."

"Yeah…maybe. But I don't know what to do. I'm stuck. Even without the issue of my family, I still don't see a future with him. That tells me I should leave soon so I won't have any regrets later down the line."

"Why don't you see a future with him?"

"Because I want a marriage and a family, and he's so devoted to his work I don't see that happening. The safest place in the world is by his side, but it can also be dangerous. I never would have met The Butcher if I weren't exposed to that lifestyle. I don't judge Bosco for what he does for a living, but I want nothing to do with that part of his life. He would never give that up, and he shouldn't have to give it up either. That's his whole life."

Vanessa nodded in agreement. "So it sounds like it can't work anyway."

"No…it can't. As much as I don't want to say good-bye, I know I have to. If I wait too long, it'll just be harder. It'll take longer to get over him. It'll take longer to find the right man, one who wants the same things I want."

Vanessa was quiet for a long time, staring at her hands as she considered what she would say next. "I know I should keep my mouth shut, but…have you ever actually asked him?"

"Asked him what?"

"If he would want those things. If he would give up the casino to have those things."

"No…but I don't need to. He's passionate about what he does. I see it written all over his face."

Vanessa didn't push it any further. "Then enjoy the rest of your time with him. That's only three weeks away, so I'm sure our family won't find out in the meantime."

"Probably not." My heart filled with dread as I imagined the moment when I grabbed my bags and walked out. I didn't want to turn my back on this man, but I had no other choice. We were from different worlds, and no amount of love would change that. "You'll keep my secret?"

She smiled. "You know I'll always keep your secret."

———

BOSCO WAS IN HIS BOXERS WHEN I WALKED THROUGH the door, his muscled thighs chiseled from stone. Every single inch of his body was gorgeous, from his beautiful tanned skin to the perfect lines in the grooves between his muscles. Nothing compared to that handsome face, the hard jaw and soft eyes. He was the man of my dreams, the most beautiful man I'd ever had between my legs. Even if I found another man I loved, he still wouldn't compare to Bosco Roth.

He left the couch and walked up to me, giving me a kiss on the mouth while his large hands cupped the feminine curves of my body. He squeezed me in different places, touching my shoulders then my hips. His mouth continued to move against mine, soft one minute then hard the next.

I wished I could be greeted that way every day for the rest of my life.

He ended the embrace then examined my swollen eye. "Vanessa didn't think I was responsible, right?"

Actually, she did. "No. I told her what happened."

His fingertips lightly touched the area. "It's getting better." He pressed his soft lips to my injury and kissed it gently, trying to heal me with his love.

I closed my eyes as I enjoyed him, the pain immediately decreasing when his love surrounded me. My fingers explored his chest, feeling his chiseled lines and hard grooves. He was warm to the touch, comforting in comparison to the winter weather outside.

His lips moved to my ear. "Hungry?"

The last thing I wanted was food. "No." I cupped his cheeks and directed his stare to mine. "I want you to make love to me."

His eyes danced with a hint of arousal, and his hand slid into my hair with a bit of aggression, as if I'd just said the magic words. "Your wish is my command." He lifted me into the air and carried me to the couch, the closest piece of furniture that could hold both of us. He laid me down before he pulled off my shoes, jeans, and thong. He left everything above the waist on, only interested in what was below the hips. He pushed his boxers down next and revealed his pulsating cock, the biggest dick I'd ever fucked. He wrapped his fingers around his length and pumped a few times before he settled between my legs. He propped one of my legs over the back of the couch and pinned the other back, making my foot press against the coffee table. I was open far and wide, and he slid inside without any objection.

My palms pressed against his chest, and I looked into his eyes as he started to move. My conversation with Vanessa was forgotten as I watched this man make love to me. His powerful body worked hard to pump inside me, and the sex noises our bodies made together filled the living room. The smell of dinner was in the air, but neither one of us cared about the food that was ready to be eaten.

All we cared about was this.

"Babe, right there." My nails clawed into his ass, and I guided him to the right spot, the button that was making my legs shake.

He moaned when I said his nickname. His eyes always reacted when I said it because he never got used to it. His hands dug into my hair, and then he kissed me, giving me a slow embrace that matched his deep and even strokes. He breathed into my mouth before he whispered to me, "I love you, Beautiful." He pumped into me three times. "Fuck, I love you."

I didn't fight it anymore. When I felt the love inside my chest, I let it out. "Babe, I love you so much...so damn much."

BOSCO AND I DIDN'T TALK ABOUT THE FUTURE OF our relationship again. He seemed confident that I wouldn't leave, that the three-month mark would come and go without consequence. That put him in a good mood, loving and devoted any time I walked through the door. He seemed to be softer than he used to be, more relaxed now that he let out the feelings he'd been harboring inside his chest. He was distinctly different toward me than he was with everyone else, even Ronan. He was his rough and cold self all the same.

When I came home from work, he was dressed in a full suit.

That only meant one thing. He was going to work.

I hated the nights he was gone from the penthouse. It forced me to stay up way later than I would like, watching mindless TV while I waited for the elevator to beep with his arrival. Just that alone was enough reason we didn't have a future together. If I were home with our children, I would never feel safe if he was gone all night. I would feel even more vulnerable taking care of our kids without him there to protect all of us.

It would never work.

Bosco wore that lopsided grin. "Bad day?"

"No. But I'm about to have a bad night." I grabbed his tie and pulled him in for a kiss, smothering him with affection the way a wife would smother her husband. "It would be amazing if you were home by midnight. Two or three in the morning is just unbearable."

"I'm not working tonight."

"Then where are you going?"

"We are going to dinner. I put a dress for you on the bed."

The two of us never went out anywhere. We had all our meals at the penthouse and spent our time screwing and talking. "Dinner?"

"Yes. I want to take you out."

The upside to that was I could order whatever I wanted, like something covered in cheese. The downside to that was being in public. I didn't want to be seen with Bosco anywhere, just in case someone recognized me. "Where are we going?"

"Giovanni's."

That wasn't a restaurant that had a distribution relationship with the winery, so it was probably safe. The people there shouldn't know my father. "Alright. Let me change." I kissed him again just because I enjoyed it so much before I walked into the bedroom and changed. I slipped on the heels sitting out for me and pulled on the deep blue dress. I fixed my makeup and hair then walked to the elevator.

Bosco opened a large black coat and wrapped it around me. The buttons were made of shiny gold, and he buttoned each one to make sure I was warm in the twenty pounds of cotton that he wrapped around me. He took my hand and pulled me into the elevator.

After we were out into the garage, we got into the back seat of his car and hit the road. Two cars followed behind us, and another two were in the front. I wouldn't be surprised if Bosco decided to add two tanks to his ranks.

"Can I make a request?"

He was looking out the window, but he pulled his gaze away to look at me. "Always."

"Can we not shut down the restaurant?"

The corner of his mouth rose in a smile. "Still not a fan?"

"I think it's obnoxious to ruin other people's nights just because you think you're more important than everyone else."

"I am more important." He said it without apology, not caring what I thought of the statement. "And you're even more important than me."

"Even if that were true, I don't want to do that." I knew I had a lot of power in this relationship now that I had his heart in my palm. I could make demands that would always be met. "So we aren't clearing out the restaurant."

He wore the same gaze, neither angry nor impressed. Finally, he gave a subtle nod. "Whatever you want, Beautiful." He looked out the window again.

I won the round but didn't gloat. I wasn't looking forward to displaying a black eye in a crowded restaurant, but I didn't care what anyone thought of us. I did my best to cover it with makeup, but there was no amount of foundation that could hide the bright purple color completely surrounding my eye. That man hit me with considerable force, making the inside of my eye darker than a black hole.

We pulled up to the restaurant and walked inside, my hand tucked inside Bosco's. All he did was look at the man standing at the podium, and he immediately got the service he wanted. Everyone else waiting for a table was ignored.

"Shall I clear out the restaurant, sir?"

"Unnecessary. Just a private table please."

We were immediately guided to the corner where we had some space from everyone else. Bosco pulled out my chair for me then sat across from me. We were near one of the windows, and just outside I could see one of Bosco's cars parked there, so they could keep an eye on the man who paid their bills.

Bosco ordered a bottle of wine for the table.

"You don't have to order Barsetti wine every time because of me."

He looked at his menu. "I realize that. I genuinely enjoy it." As if he'd finished his selections, he shut the menu. "I respect the harvest they produce every year. Other wineries sometimes compromise on quality to meet demand, but the Barsettis never do. They pride themselves on what they do, because legacy and respect are more important than money."

It was nice to hear a compliment about my family for once. "You described my father and uncle perfectly."

"They're good business owners—regardless of what

their product is." He sat perfectly upright in his chair then stared at me openly, his favorite pastime.

I looked at my menu.

"What are you getting?"

"Lasagna. You?"

"Caprese salad with chicken."

I made a gagging noise. "We're at dinner. Get something good."

"That is good."

"Uh, no. I'm the one who should be eating a salad, and hell no, that's not gonna happen."

"What's that supposed to mean?" he asked, his eyes narrowing. "You do not need to eat a salad."

"That's not what I meant. I just mean usually women are the ones who order lame stuff like that. Come on, we're out on a date. Consider it to be your cheat day."

He smiled again, amused by my stance. "Then what do you suggest? How about the chicken with—"

"Spaghetti. Get the spaghetti."

He chuckled. "Alright."

"Good. You're gonna look sexy as hell when we get home regardless."

He must have loved everything I said in that sentence because his smile vanished and his eyes turned intense.

The waiter came by and took our order before he disappeared again. Our table had a vase with a single red rose and a white candle that flickered. The other tables were filled with couples of all different ages, enjoying their time out. There was no other man in that restaurant who could compare to Bosco. But then again, there was no other man in the world who could compare to him. When I started seeing someone else, I would have a hard time not looking back on these memories, remembering times like these.

Bosco kept watching me, entertained by my expression just as other people were entertained by TV. He wasn't wearing his poker face like he did around everyone else. This look was completely transparent— just intense.

I should be used to the stare by now, but I wasn't. No man had ever looked at me that way before, like he owned me in a way no one else ever would. He didn't wear his heart on his sleeve, but in his eyes. We were surrounded by people, but it seemed like I was the only woman in the room. He was immune to Ruby's charms because he was obsessed with mine.

"What are you thinking?" I asked.

"You don't want to know." His voice wasn't full of threat, and it didn't seem like his words meant anything sinister.

My curiosity forced my hand. "I do."

"I was regretting my choice to dine with the public. If they weren't here, I could be fucking you on this table right now. Or even against the window. So many options…"

Only he could pull off a statement like that and

arouse a woman. I pictured those positions, my dress hiked up and his pants pushed far enough down so he could slip his dick inside me. I'd always been a sexual woman, but I'd never been as aroused as I was with him. With Bosco Roth, I wanted it all the time. "I could always crawl beneath the table and suck you off under the tablecloth."

He clearly hadn't been expecting an answer like that, because his eyes widened slightly and his jaw clenched. It was the same look he wore when he was angry, but this time, it was because he was so aroused he didn't know how to react. Stunned and still, he continued to drill his eyes into my face.

I grabbed my glass and drank my wine, licking my lips when I was finished.

He still didn't move. His chest didn't even rise with his breathing. "Beautiful, I love you."

3

CANE

I SAT in my office at the second winery, the fifty-acre plot of land Crow and I bought thirty years ago to keep the business growing. The phone was pressed to my ear as I listened to my grandson talk.

"And then Grandma took me to the zoo to see the giraffes. I was hoping to see dinosaurs…but they didn't have any." His voice trailed away in sadness.

I tried not to laugh, finding this young guy beautiful and amusing. "Keep looking. Maybe you'll find them someday."

"Yeah," Luca said. "And then we got ice cream. I'm not supposed to have ice cream before dinner, but Grandma says she can do whatever she wants."

I laughed. "Yeah, that sounds about right. She says the same thing to me every day."

"Grandma wants to talk to you again. Bye, Grandpa."

"Bye, Luca. Love you."

"Love you too."

Adelina came back on the phone. "He's got so much energy, huh?" she said with a laugh.

"Yes, *Bellissima*." I didn't expect to have a grandchild so soon, let alone one who was almost ten years old, but Luca had become a part of the Barsetti family overnight. *Bellissima* and I saw him as our son's son, not caring if he had a father none of us would ever meet. We loved him with all our hearts. It was love at first sight for me. "Having a good day?"

"Yes." She sighed into the phone. "I just don't want to give him back…"

"*Bellissima*, I'm sure we'll babysit all the time. Carter likes to travel, and I bet Mia would love to see the world."

"But I'm sure they want to take him with them, unfortunately. I miss having kids, Cane. I want to have more."

I couldn't tell if she was joking or not. "We're gonna have a lot of grandkids. Carmen will meet the right guy before you know it."

"I hope so. She's seeing someone now. She claims it's not serious, but it seems like it is. I'm never sure with her."

The last thing I wanted to think about was my daughter's dating life. I just wanted her to find a husband, a great guy, and that be the end of it. Once she was married, I wouldn't have to worry about her anymore, and she could have lots of kids and be happy. "When she's found someone worth talking about, she'll talk about it." My phone started to beep in my ear because there was someone on the other line. "*Bellissima*, I have to go. I'll talk to you when I get home."

"Alright. Love you."

"Love you too." I ended the call and switched lines, readopting my cold tone. "Barsetti." So many people called me that I didn't always know who was trying to contact me, so that was how I answered the phone unless it was family.

"Hey, Mr. Barsetti. It's Tomas from Giovanni's."

Giovanni's was a restaurant in Florence. We recently struck a deal to supply them wine for the restaurant. It was a new relationship, but so far, it'd been going smoothly. "Hey, how are you? I hope you aren't increasing your shipment because we're low at the moment. You know, with tourist season just around the corner."

"No, it's not about business." He suddenly turned quiet, like he didn't know how to continue this conversation. Tomas and I weren't close because we'd just met about a week ago. He came into my office, complimented a picture of my family, and we started a partnership. But other than that, very little was said. "I don't know how to say this...but from one father to another, I thought I should tell you."

I didn't like that one bit. The only kid I had in

Florence was Carmen, so I suspected this had something to do with her. "Tomas, what is it?" I leaned
forward over my desk, the phone pressed a little harder
to my ear.

"Your daughter was in here last night."

What was the big deal about that? "Okay…"

He sighed again, like this was the most painful
conversation he'd ever had. "You know who Bosco Roth
is, I take it?"

He was the biggest crime lord in Europe, operating
an illegal casino in plain sight. He was the only man in
the country who operated a fight ring, making men fight
to the death as punishment and sport. He was rumored
to be cruel but fair. But he was also said to be a loose
cannon. "Not by acquaintance, but by reputation."

"Well, your daughter had dinner with him
last night."

Like someone had punched me with brass knuckles,
the air left my lungs as well as my stomach. I knew
Bosco's face, so I pictured him sitting across from
Carmen, a maniac who probably thought she could be
bought. He employed strippers and whores at his
casino, so he obviously had no respect for women—let
alone my daughter. I couldn't speak because the rage
was building inside me, spilling over like lava from a
volcano.

"The context was clearly romantic. They arrived in
a car together and left in the same car."

Fuck.

"Worst part is…she had a black eye."

The second those words were out of his mouth, I couldn't think logically. My little girl, the beautiful baby that once fit in my arms, had been struck by a man who thought he had the power to do whatever he wanted. He touched my daughter—and he would pay the price. I didn't say goodbye to Tomas or thank him for giving me this information. I hung up and took off.

CROW AND GRIFFIN WERE IN THE OFFICE WHEN I walked inside, going over shipment orders and other bullshit. With a rifle swung over my back and two pistols in my holsters, I was prepared for war.

Crow normally ignored my outbursts, but when he saw me walking around armed in broad daylight, he didn't ignore it. "What is it?" He tossed the papers aside and stood up, fishing his gun out of one of his drawers. What I liked most about my brother was he was always prepared for a fight. He rose to any challenge and never backed down.

Griffin rose to his feet as well, eyeing my guns without flinching. Muscled and thick, he was a good man to join the team. I would need all the help I could get.

"One of my guys just told me Carmen had dinner with Bosco Roth last night."

Crow's eyes snapped open farther, recognizing that

name as well as I did. Bosco had come into power ten years ago, and it was frightening how quickly the young man had overtaken the city. It wouldn't have been possible without us because when we disrupted the chain of power when we killed Bones Sr. and dismantled the Skull Kings. But Bosco took the opportunity—and thrived.

Griffin took a deep breath, but he didn't seem as angry as Crow was.

"Fuck," Crow said. "Of all the men in the world…"

"That's not the worst part," I continued, out of breath because of my fury, not from running around all over the place. "He said she had a black eye."

Now Crow's ferocity matched mine, and he was ready to put Bosco in the ground like I was. He grabbed his pistol and cocked it. "Then he must die."

That was exactly what I was looking for.

Griffin continued to stay silent.

"I say we hunt him down, get a clean shot, and shoot him right between the eyes." I wanted that fucker dead. I wanted to take his body and shove it inside a sewer drain. I wanted him to suffer a million times more than Carmen ever had.

"Cane, this guy isn't like our other enemies," my brother said. "He's the most ruthless—"

"There's something I need to say." Griffin finally spoke up, tense but not furious. "You aren't going to like what I have to tell you. I understand if you hate me all over again, but keep in mind that my loyalties were divided."

I turned to him, having no idea what this was about. "Griffin, what the hell are you talking about?"

"Yeah," Crow said. "Speak."

"The black eye she's sporting isn't from him." He slid his hands into the pockets of his jeans, wearing a remorseful expression despite how powerful he looked. "From what I understand, he's never hurt her or laid a hand on her."

My eyes burned into his when I began to understand the situation. "You knew about this…"

"Yes," he admitted, his voice still strong. "I knew."

My hand shook because I wanted to beat the butt of the gun into his cheek.

My brother noticed my tremors. "Cane." That was all he needed to say to remind me to restrain myself.

"This is what happened," Griffin said. "Vanessa and I had dinner with Carmen one night. I always offer to take her home, but since Vanessa was tired and cold, Carmen insisted on walking alone. Apparently, four guys got her in an alleyway—"

"Stop." I couldn't listen to this. I was tough and unbreakable, but this was something I couldn't handle.

Crow finished for me. "Get to the point, Griffin."

"Alright," Griffin said. "Bosco was walking by when it happened. He intervened and saved her. She wasn't hurt in the ordeal. She held her own pretty well, actually."

"He's not the kind of guy to save a random woman," I noted.

"He's not," Griffin said in agreement. "But he owed me a favor. She name-dropped me in the alleyway, and that's why he chased them off. That's when they met. I guess he asked her out to dinner, and that's how their relationship started."

Relationship. They had a relationship. "God…no."

"Vanessa was the only person she told. Vanessa kept Carmen's secret, even from me." Griffin's shoulders tensed before he kept talking. "I guess it was casual, but then things became more serious. When things became too complicated, Carmen tried to break it off. He wouldn't allow it."

Now I was flying apart at the hinges. "I'm gonna shoot this motherfucker and put him in the fucking—"

"Cane." Crow held his hand up to me. "If you can't handle this, then you need to step outside. If we're gonna help Carmen, we need to know everything. Alright? So chill."

"Easy for you to say," I hissed. "This isn't your daughter."

"She's as good as," Crow said coldly. "I'd die for her, and we both know it. So stop taking this out on me and just shut up." He turned back to Griffin. "What else?"

Griffin continued. "So they negotiated a three-month relationship. She's living with him at his penthouse. The only reason I found out was because I checked on her when the shop was closed, so I went to her apartment, but it was obvious she hadn't been there in months. I found her car at his place and made the connection. That same night, Bosco showed up on my doorstep for a chat."

"Shit," Crow said. "What happened? Vanessa?"

"He called me from the road, and I met him outside the gate," Griffin said. "Vanessa doesn't even know it happened. He came unarmed and without his army. He just wanted to chat. It wasn't hostile."

"And what did this motherfucker say?" I asked through clenched teeth.

"He told me he would never hurt her. That he cares about her. He assured me that when their time together is over, she can walk away. She's not a prisoner. But he did threaten to kill all of us if we try to oppose him." Griffin lowered himself back into his seat, his elbows on his knees. "You know I would die for Barsetti blood. I've already proven it to you, so it goes without saying. But Bosco Roth is a whole different animal. He's not a regular thug. This guy has a hundred armed men at his side at any given time of the day. He has every criminal in this vicinity under his thumb. If you're on his list… you don't stand a chance."

That wasn't what I wanted to hear.

"He's right," Crow admitted. "This isn't a clean strike. There's little chance of success."

"No chance of success," Griffin corrected. "None at all."

I refused to accept that. "This is my daughter, and I

will die to protect her. I would rather be in the ground than alive knowing she's in trouble."

Griffin shook his head. "After Bosco and I talked, I confronted her about it. She insists he's kind, generous, and loving. He treats her with respect, keeps her safe, and takes care of her. She defended him in every single instance and even claimed he was a good man. She understands his reputation, but he's different with her. She said she's not a prisoner, and she can walk away whenever she wants. And more importantly, their agreement ends in three more weeks. When that time comes, she said she'll leave."

Finally, some good news.

Crow continued to stand behind his desk, but he put the safety on his gun and set it down. "If he's such a great guy, why does she want to leave?"

"Said she doesn't see a future with him," Griffin said. "She wants a husband and kids, but that's not gonna happen with him. She wants a simple life in Tuscany, and since he's so involved in his work, it's not possible. Also…she knows you guys would never be on board with this."

"Looks like my daughter isn't that dumb, after all," I said bitterly.

Crow gave me a look of disapproval. "Cane, don't do that."

"I'm pissed," I snapped. "I'm pissed that my daughter was stupid enough to get mixed up in this."

Crow sat down in his leather chair. "Griffin just said

she likes the guy. He's good to her. She can leave whenever she wants. I'm not happy about this, but it could be a lot worse."

I shook my head. "This is as bad as it could get. I don't want my daughter anywhere near him."

"I don't like him either," Griffin said. "But he looked me in the eye and said he does nothing but treat her with respect. He's not a liar, so I believe him."

"Fuck." I sat down and ran my hands through my hair. "This is a nightmare."

"I would have done something if she were in real danger," Griffin said. "But since it's gonna be over in three weeks, and she actually likes the guy…I decided it was riskier to do something."

Three weeks was too long for me. "I don't want that asshole anywhere near my daughter. Whether you're with me or not, I have to do something."

My brother looked at me. "Cane——"

"I don't care if Carmen likes the guy. She's been brainwashed. And what if the three weeks ends, and he changes his mind?"

Crow didn't have a response to that.

"He said that wouldn't happen," Griffin said.

"And you believe him?" I asked incredulously.

"Yes," Griffin said. "And Carmen does too. I don't like this any more than you do, but I feel like there's nothing we can do. Carmen seems to have a close relationship with him. She says she can walk away now if she wanted to."

"I don't care," I said. "That's not even something you should say in a relationship."

Crow turned to Griffin. "How did she get the black eye?"

"She was at that bank when it was robbed," Griffin said. "One of the guys punched her."

"Jesus Christ." I covered my face with both my hands and actually felt the desire to weep. This whole time I thought my little girl was safe living on her own, and now I knew she was being terrorized in alleyways, dominated by a crime lord, and mugged at the bank.

"Bosco's men handled it. Killed the men and saved her," Griffin finished. "In her eyes, he's saved her life three times."

"When was the third?" Crow asked. "You only mentioned two."

"I guess one of the men at the casino became obsessed with her," Griffin said. "Started stalking her. Bosco threw him in the ring, but he beat his competitor. So Bosco jumped in and finished the match himself. Broke his arm and his back. The man pleaded for mercy, and Bosco shot him."

This man was a million times worse than I ever could have imagined. Not only was he powerful, but he wasn't afraid to bloody his knuckles either. He didn't have to jump in the ring, but he did it anyway—just to prove how strong he was. "I don't know what to do." If I could march down there and blow his head off, I would, but I wasn't stupid. I would never make it past his army and his security. The man never went anywhere alone, so there was no possibility of success. "I guess I should talk to Carmen myself."

"I don't think that's a good idea," Griffin said. "It's not going to change anything, and she said she would keep this a secret from you."

"Then what are you suggesting?" I snapped. "Just forget the whole thing and be fine with it?"

"Fighting him isn't an option," Crow said. "It's a suicide mission."

"But this is my daughter," I reminded him. "Saving Conway was a suicide mission, and I was still there."

"But we still had a chance," Crow said. "This is totally different. He's the worst opponent we could possibly face."

"I don't give a shit," I said. "This is my daughter. I'll do anything for her."

"Cane." Griffin shook his head. "Carmen wouldn't want you to get yourself killed. It wouldn't help her anyway—especially since she wants to be with him."

"Like I said, she's confused," I hissed.

"I agree with Griffin," Crow said. "Fighting him will get us nowhere. Just dead in a ditch. We wouldn't be doing our family any favors by all of us dying."

I was too angry to think straight. I just wanted my daughter to be out of this situation, to make sure this man wasn't brainwashing her or forcing her to do something she didn't want to do. The fact that all these terrible things had happened to her made my heart break into a million pieces. Just because Bosco was the richest man in the country didn't mean he could get away with this. The thought gave me an idea. "All he cares about is money."

Griffin lifted his gaze to meet mine. "What?"

"All he cares about is money," I repeated. "If we walk in there with a hundred million in cash, that might get him to forget about Carmen. That's a lot of money, even to someone like him. We tell him it's his if he just forgets about her."

Crow didn't shoot the idea down right away. He looked to Griffin next.

Griffin considered it for a long time. "If we threaten him, we're subjecting ourselves to a battle we can't win. But if we try to buy him off…that is a better approach. He might go for it, but I'm not sure."

At least we finally had a plan—a plan to save my daughter.

WE ALL SNUCK OUT OF THE HOUSE SO THE WIVES wouldn't worry. If *Bellissima* knew about this…she would lose her mind. We met at the winery, piling our leather bags of money into the back of the truck.

We left the guns in the bed of the truck since we couldn't bring them inside. There was no point in trying to sneak anything in because Bosco's men would find them anyway. We were going through the tightest security in this country, and it was stupid to think we would fool them.

Crow was there because he would follow me into hell, not just because I helped him with Conway and Vanessa. He was the one person I could always count on. He had my back until time claimed both of our bodies. "I want Griffin to stay behind."

Griffin turned to him, his expression cold and fierce, but his surprise still obvious.

"Why?" I asked, preferring Griffin's company since he was the strongest of the three of us.

"If we don't make it back, I feel comfortable knowing he'll protect my wife and daughter." Crow spoke highly of his son-in-law even though he used to do just the opposite. He gave him respect instead of hatred, and it was his idea to hand the winery down to him—which I'd agreed to.

"He's the strongest of the three of us. I feel more comfortable having him around." I wasn't ashamed to admit that. Crow and I were still tough men, but we were nothing compared to how we used to be in our youth. Griffin didn't just surpass us in power, but in youth. "We're going into the underworld. All we have is our reputation, which has grown stale. Griffin is at least current."

"I want to be there," Griffin said. "Carmen means a lot to me."

I'd noticed Griffin's affection for my daughter a long time ago. It wasn't sleazy, but brotherly.

"He is the strongest of us," Crow said in agreement. "Which is why I want him to stay behind. He's the second line of defense if something bad happens. He's more capable than our sons, and he has connections. He'll handle the winery and become the patriarch of the family. Cane, he has to stay."

Griffin looked at the ground, but his body relaxed like those words meant something to him.

I couldn't argue with my brother's reasoning. "Alright. It's just us, then. Let's do this."

WE KNEW EXACTLY WHERE THE CASINO WAS BECAUSE it was in plain sight. Bosco didn't fear the police or private law enforcement. They were powerless against a man like him. So they were allowed to break the law every day, keeping the peace in exchange for law enforcement's cooperation.

We had a few men accompany us, but that was just to carry the bags of cash. None of them were armed.

We approached the side entrance and stepped inside, immediately drawing attention because they recognized our faces but knew we weren't members of the casino. They searched us, finding nothing but our phones. They looked at the money next and didn't blink an eye when they saw all the cash tucked away inside the leather bags. But they put the bags on the conveyor belt of the X-ray machine to make sure there was nothing hidden in the stacks of bills.

They were extremely thorough.

Once everything was in order, the man in charge of the security floor addressed both of us. "What do you want? This is way too much for membership dues, so you must have another intention." His hands came together at his waist, his pistol sitting on his hip. The rest of the men were dressed in suits and held rifles. There were at least twelve of them on this floor alone.

I wasn't intimidated, probably because I was blinded by my love for Carmen. All I cared about was protecting her, getting her away from this asshole. I would make any sacrifice for that to happen. "I want to speak to Bosco alone."

The man stared at me with his brown eyes, looking uninterested despite the words I just said. "Why?"

"That's my business, not yours." Being difficult wouldn't get me anywhere, but I wouldn't bow down like some kind of pussy. "You're paid to wipe his ass, not be involved in his personal affairs. Tell him the Barsetti brothers want to see him. He'll know exactly what it's about."

Crow kept his stern expression beside me, seeming unafraid of the armed men surrounding us. They could blow our brains out with all their weapons and keep the cash, but since Bosco paid their bills, they wouldn't do a damn thing until he gave the order.

The man's eyes narrowed in offense, and he held my

gaze for a long time, like he wished there was something he could do in retaliation. Unfortunately for him, there wasn't. So he stepped into a different room and left us alone with the remaining eleven men.

Minutes passed.

Crow and I stood side by side but didn't exchange a single word. We didn't give away our motivations, just in case there were cameras watching every move we made. I crossed my arms over my chest and seemed bored, while my brother stared at the wall ahead, looking unconcerned with the whole situation.

It wasn't until fifteen minutes had passed before the man returned. "Your men stay outside. We'll escort you to Bosco along with the money." He nodded to his men. A few took up a formation around us, while the others grabbed the bags of money and carried them for us.

We moved through a few doors before we finally entered the casino.

Another dozen armed men surrounded us, cutting us off from socializing with anyone else in the room. It may have looked like they were protecting us, but they were keeping us isolated from everyone and everything in the room, just in case we had a trick up our sleeve.

At least Bosco Roth didn't underestimate us.

We moved to the other side of the floor and stopped in front of double red doors. There were no tables or members around the area, so it seemed like it was off-limits. The man in charge opened the doors and ushered us into a private lounge with a full bar. There were two leather sofas in the center of the room, and the lighting was moody and dark. A bartender was behind the counter.

Bosco Roth sat on the leather sofa facing us, wearing a black suit and matching tie. He met our gaze without flinching, as if he was indifferent to our sudden appearance on his turf. His elbows rested on his thighs, and he stared at us with striking blue eyes that were similar to Griffin's. A glass of scotch was on the table, and he took a drink as he stared at us.

The men piled the bags of money in the corner.

Four men took their places around the room, holding their rifles. The others left.

Crow and I stood behind the other couch, staring at our enemy as I tried to gauge more about this powerful man. Just looking at him pissed me off, that smug gaze and that expensive suit. He thought he owned the world. He thought he owned my daughter.

I wanted nothing more than to take one of those rifles, put the barrel in his mouth, and pull the trigger.

Bosco didn't rise. "Take a seat, gentlemen."

I didn't want to cooperate simply because I hated him. I wanted to be disobedient, to disrespect him as much as possible.

Bosco barely waved his hand before the bartender was at his side. "Get these gentlemen whatever they would like."

"Yes, sir." He came to Crow first. "What will you be drinking this evening?"

"Scotch—on the rocks," Crow answered.

The bartender turned to me next, asking the question with just his gaze.

"I don't want anything from this asshole."

The bartender didn't react before he walked away.

Bosco held my gaze, not even slightly offended.

The bartender placed Crow's drink on the table then resumed his position behind the bar.

Crow moved to the couch, so I followed suit. We sat down and faced Bosco, the table was the only piece of furniture between us.

Bosco seemed comfortable in his element, surrounded by booze, men, and power. He had the upper hand in the situation, and he knew it. He wasn't afraid of us—and it didn't seem like he was pretending. He grabbed his glass and took a drink, licking his lips when he was finished. "It's smooth. You should try some, Cane."

I ground my teeth together, despising his arrogance. "I'm about to knock your teeth out."

All the men pointed their rifles right at me. It suddenly became very tense, the silence deafening because of the threat lingering in the air. My brother didn't undermine me in front of Bosco by telling me to calm down, even though that was probably what he was thinking.

Bosco gave a subtle wave of his hand, and the men immediately pointed their rifles to the ground once more. He kept his gaze on me the entire time, knowing the men would obey without having to check. "Who should go first? Me or you?" He maintained a calm persona, which gave him more power in the situation. He had complete control over this city, so our visit was uneventful to him. He didn't feel the need to control the conversation because it didn't matter. He would win either way.

"I'll get right to the point, asshole." I refused to call him by his name, especially to his face. He didn't deserve that respect. He could shoot me if he wanted to.

Bosco didn't flinch at the insult. "Alright. What's the point?"

"I brought a hundred million with me tonight. Your men counted it. It's not counterfeit."

He chuckled slightly, like that was amusing. "The Barsettis have a respectable reputation. They wouldn't pull an idiotic stunt like that. I know you're good for it." He grabbed his glass and took another drink. "I'm flattered you think a membership is that expensive, but you're a hundred times over the asking price."

Fucking prick. "The money is yours. Just let my daughter go."

"Let her go?" He raised an eyebrow, his fingertips on the top of the glass. "She's not a prisoner, Cane. That woman can do whatever she wants."

"You know what I mean." My body was still, only because I was focused so deeply on the conversation. My anger made me want to shake, made me want to tighten my hands into fists so I could break his jaw. Bosco was a handsome man with attractive features, from his strong jawline, fit physique, and bright eyes. There was nothing I wanted more than to beat him bloody. "A hundred million is yours—if you drop her. That's a hundred memberships. Even to a man as rich as you, that's serious cash. Forget about her, and find someone else to keep you entertained."

He stared at me with frost in his eyes, like my offer actually offended him. "Carmen Barsetti is worth more than a hundred million. She's worth more than all the money in the world—because she's invaluable. You could offer me a billion, and my answer would be the same—*no*."

I had to stop myself from grabbing his drink and smashing the tumbler over his head. I wanted to shove a shard of glass deep into his eyes and make him permanently blind. I would be dead shortly afterward so I wouldn't be able to enjoy it, but that didn't matter. I didn't care about the rest of my family because I cared so much about my only daughter.

"When Carmen told me her family would never accept me, I assumed it was an exaggeration." He chuckled, mostly to himself. "But damn, she wasn't kidding. I never imagined you would walk right up to my doorstep and try to buy me off—without saying a word to her. The Barsetti men are as controlling as the rumors say."

"Then what's it gonna take?" I asked, ignoring

everything he said. "How do I get rid of you? What's your price?"

He held his glass in his palm, his fingertips lightly tapping against the side. "Why do you want to get rid of me so badly? What's so terrible about me, Cane? From my vantage point, it seems like I'm excessively rich, unquestionably powerful, and surprisingly generous."

"Generous?" I asked.

"Because you're still alive." The room turned ice-cold around us, like the temperature dropped to freezing. "You haven't given me a chance whatsoever. Your daughter is my woman because she wants to be. Not because she has to or because she's working off some kind of debt." He glanced at my brother, referring to Pearl. "I keep her safe. I give her anything she could possibly want. Instead of barging in here and trying to sabotage our relationship, perhaps you should have spoken to your daughter and listened to her. Give her a chance to explain how she feels about me. Get all the facts. Don't come in here and try to rip us apart. Would you really want that for your daughter? For me to take the money and then break her heart?" He moved closer to me. "Would you really do that to her?"

I held his gaze, unafraid of his proximity. "I'm protecting my daughter. And I will go to any lengths to make that happen."

He sat back again and refilled his glass. "I believe you love your daughter. And I believe she loves you— because she tells me often. She speaks highly of you—

all of you. For that reason, I'm not going to tell her about this conversation. She would be very disappointed if she knew her father, the man she admires the most, marched down here and interfered in her personal life. You forget that she's a grown woman who's capable of making her own decisions."

I was touched by what he said, but I refused to show it. "She's obviously incapable of making good decisions if she's involved with *you*."

He held his glass without taking a drink. "The two of you used to sell weapons to criminals and terrorists. Crow's son-in-law was a hitman. Your son bought a woman from the underground then made her his wife. The list goes on…" He shook his head slightly. "My crimes are petty compared to yours. I run a business —that's it."

"You're involved with murderers and rapists on a daily basis," I snapped. "I don't want my daughter around that. I want her to be safe. We've all walked away from those lives to keep our family safe."

"There's nowhere safer in the world than by my side," Bosco countered. "She has twelve men guarding her at any given time. They blend in with her surroundings, but they're prepared to intervene if a man simply looks at her too long. If it weren't for me, you would have lost your daughter months ago when she was taken down that alleyway. You would have lost her at the bank. I'm the monster that keeps the other monsters at bay—let's not pretend otherwise. When one of the men from the casino became obsessed with her, I took care of it. Instead of having my men shoot him in the back of the head, I did it myself—with my bare hands." He held up one hand and made a fist. "I have proved a million times over that I can be the man your daughter deserves. Instead of immediately dismissing me, you should have the humility to give me a chance—have a fucking drink with me." He slammed his glass down, making it thud loudly. "I don't want to come between you and your daughter, so your secret is safe with me. But I hope you don't repeat your brother's mistakes." He glanced at Crow before turning back to me.

"If you're such a good guy, why is there a three-month arrangement?" Crow questioned, speaking for the first time. "And from what we understand, she tried to leave, and you wouldn't allow it. Doesn't sound like you're the nice guy you claim to be."

Bosco took his time before he answered, absorbing the question like a sponge. "The only reason Carmen has ever pushed me away is because she didn't see a future—because you two would never approve. I asked her to give me a real chance. That's all I ever wanted. When she finally did…we had something beautiful."

"You didn't answer my question, asshole." My eyes narrowed on his face, hating the way he danced around my question.

No matter how many times I insulted him, he never grew angry. "I'm not the same man I used to be. I'm much different now from the moment we met. I won't pretend I was some kind of gentleman who played by the rules. But your daughter has softened me in many good ways. I need you to understand that I would never hurt her, that I only want to make her happy, and her safety is my priority."

A part of me believed him when I didn't want to. I was deep inside his lair, and he could have killed us a while ago. It wouldn't be difficult to cover this up, especially when Griffin was the only one who knew what was happening.

"I'll be frank with you, Cane," Bosco continued. "Carmen has told me, many times, that her family is the most important thing to her. If the Barsettis will never accept me, then there's no hope for us. I respect that because I respect everything that comes out of her pretty mouth. She doesn't settle for less than what she deserves, and she's not afraid to stand up for what she believes in. You raised a fine daughter—independent, smart, and resourceful. If that moment comes, and she wants to leave…I'll let her go."

Finally, some good news. "You will?"

He nodded. "I already told you I respect her. I'm sorry you didn't believe that."

It was hard for me to believe anything he said, not when he had such a barbaric reputation.

"But you wouldn't be doing her any favors… because she loves me."

"She does not love you." My daughter might be

dumb enough to get into this situation, but she couldn't be that stupid.

He brought his hands together, his fingertips touching. "I told her I love her, Cane. I say it every day. And she says it back. You can think what you want, but I'm telling you the truth. I just want you to understand that this relationship isn't just physical. It's intimate, emotional, intense. It's… I can't even describe it. I would die for her in a heartbeat. By extension…I would never hurt you or your brother." He pointed his hands at me then at Crow. "Because it would hurt the woman I love. Maybe I should have kept that information to myself, but I'm putting all my cards on the table…so you can see exactly what I have in my hand."

Crow sighed quietly behind me, not in relief, but in disappointment. He turned to me, giving me a look only I would understand.

Now I realized this was so much more complicated than I had imagined. I was hoping Bosco was an asshole who was using her, so it would be easier to get rid of him. But if he loved her and she loved him…it didn't seem like I had a chance.

Bosco kept his hands together and continued to stare at me, giving me a chance to process what he'd said. "Don't do this the wrong way. Don't push away your daughter or force her to push me away. She needs both of us."

After watching Crow go through the most difficult six months of his life, I didn't want to repeat his mistakes. He pushed Vanessa away when he got rid of Griffin, and that ended up being a horrible error in judgment. Despite Griffin's past, he was a good man—and worthy of Crow's daughter.

I didn't want to do the same thing. I didn't want to put Carmen through the heartache, nor do it to myself.

Bosco waited patiently for some kind of response.

I was at a loss for words. All of this had been happening for the last three months, and now that so much time had passed, my daughter had fallen in love with the biggest crime lord I'd ever heard of.

Crow stared me for a second, pity in his eyes. He turned back to Bosco. "I think I can speak for my brother when I say he still doesn't like this. No father wants his daughter to be with a man so close to danger. My son-in-law works at the winery with us, so he's not associated with that lifestyle anymore. Even if Carmen loves you and you love her…it's not a good match."

"With all due respect, that's not for you to decide," Bosco said simply. "Carmen can make her own decisions. I'm the only man she's ever loved. She's so beautiful that she can have whatever man she wants. She obviously only wants me." He didn't put it delicately, but he wasn't abrasive either. "Despite what you may think of me, I've earned her. I'm not afraid to get my hands bloody in her honor. I would lay down my life for hers in a heartbeat. The robber at the bank gave her that black eye. So I stabbed him to death and listened to him scream. There's nothing I wouldn't do for that woman, no sacrifice too big for me to make. If that doesn't make me worthy of her…I don't know what will."

He reminded me of Griffin in a lot of ways, whether that was good or bad.

Crow spoke again. "She told Griffin she would leave you when this is over. She doesn't see you being the kind of husband that she wants."

He didn't hide the pain that danced across the surface in his eyes. "That's what she says. But I know she won't walk away. What we have is too strong. She assumes I can't be what she needs, but she's never asked. Maybe if she did…she would get the answer she wants."

"In our culture, a woman doesn't introduce a man to her father unless he's going to be her husband." When I pictured that day, I always imagined Carmen introducing me to an attractive young man with a small amount of success. He was average but kind, someone safe who would make her happy. I still hoped that would happen. "With that being said, you still have a few weeks left. If she leaves you…my problems are solved. If she stays, then I guess I'll have to deal with you then." If my daughter wasn't sure if this was the man she wanted to marry, then I didn't need to worry about it now. It was obvious that he was kind to her, that he was protective and loving. He wasn't the evil and cruel crime lord I assumed he would be. He was very tame in comparison to his reputation.

Bosco finished his glass then gave a nod. "That sounds fair. You made the right decision."

"Yes," I said. "I just hope my daughter makes the right decision as well."

Bosco gave a lopsided grin, but his eyes thudded with pain. "We shall see. Can we keep this between us? So she won't be influenced either way?"

I didn't want to tell Carmen I marched down here with the intention of killing this man. She would probably be angry with me for interfering with her personal life. I'd made the same mistakes Crow did. The only difference was Bosco was kind enough to keep it a secret. "Yes. This stays between us."

4

BOSCO

Ronan sat across from me after the Barsettis left. "Nosy, aren't they?"

I didn't appreciate the way they showed up on my doorstep, but I respected the way Cane Barsetti loved his daughter. Opposing me was a suicide mission, but he didn't hesitate because his daughter was more important than him. He knew how powerful I was. He wasn't so proud as to lie to himself about the strength of his opponent. But clearly, he thought his daughter's life was far more important than his own.

How could I hate a man so selfless?

Despite how emotional he was, he was rational. He listened to me even when he didn't want to, reasoned with me to understand the truth of the situation. When I told him I loved and cared for this daughter, he seemed to believe me.

Maybe even respect me.

Because I looked him in the eye and said I loved her. I didn't flinch or blink, meaning it from the bottom of my heart. Being loved by a powerful man like me wasn't the worst thing in the world, regardless of how I earned my money.

And it would be hypocritical for him to think otherwise.

Perhaps Crow's relationship with his son-in-law had paved the way for my success.

But Cane Barsetti was no longer the problem. It was Carmen Barsetti. She had a perfect picture in her mind of what she wanted her husband to be like. She wanted a quiet and simple life, four kids running around while she took care of them. If I couldn't offer her that, it would never work.

But maybe I was prepared to offer her that. The picture wouldn't look exactly as she imagined, but it would be as close as I could possibly make it.

I almost forgot what Ronan said. "They just care about her. I can't hate a man for that."

"Still stupid to march down here."

"They had no other choice. They can't reach me any other way, and a phone call is cowardly."

"And you aren't going to tell Carmen?"

I told her everything, but I would keep this secret to myself. I wouldn't want her to know that her father overstepped his bounds. It might create problems between them, and that's not what I wanted. She wore that diamond necklace around her throat just because he gave it to her. Her love for him was written all over her face. I was never threatened by their relationship. I just wanted to be welcome in their circle. "I think her father respects me a little."

"I doubt it's very much. You did force her at one point."

"But I was honest about it. And I was honest with my feelings now."

He grinned. "My big brother is in love. Who would have thought that would happen?"

I drank from my glass then licked my lips. "Certainly not me." I'd been with beautiful women all my life. They were lovely people with kindness in their hearts. Even the ones who wanted me for my money weren't bad. But Carmen had something the others didn't…and that was why everything changed.

"So, what now?"

Carmen was home at that very moment, waiting for me to return to the penthouse so she could finally go to sleep. Sometimes I stayed out a little later just because it made me feel more powerful. This woman was at my mercy, and I liked seeing how much she needed me. "I give her a reason to stay."

I WATCHED HER THROUGH THE WINDOW FOR A moment, seeing the way she worked in her shop. She was focused on her job, grabbing handfuls of flowers and throwing together beautiful arrangements like it wasn't a challenge at all.

My objective was to go in there and actually talk to her, but I was so entertained that I chose to stay put. I watched the way her fingertips tucked her hair behind her ear, the way her beautiful cheeks were revealed, slightly rosy from her makeup. She did her eye makeup differently today, giving it a smoky look that was innately sexy. She wore light colored jeans that were skintight, brown boots, and a loose sweater that still managed to capture her curves. She was beautiful and classy, a queen without a crown.

Minutes passed before I finally crossed the street and entered her shop. The place smelled like fresh flowers right after the rain, along with her perfume. My footsteps sounded against the tile, and I slowly moved up behind her.

She set down her shears and pulled off her gloves before she looked at me. "How may I—" Surprise entered her gaze before it quickly changed to joy. A soft smile appeared on her red lips, her eyes softening at the same time.

I pressed her against the counter and slid my hand into her hair as I kissed her. The public could watch us through the windows, but I didn't care. My hand glided up under her sweater, and I felt her tummy underneath. My cock was hard from watching her from across the street, and I wanted her to feel it, to know I wanted her all the time. My kisses moved to her neck, and I gave her soft embraces, my warm breath moving across her skin. She'd told me not to make an appearance here again, but since Griffin knew about us, there was no harm anymore. My lips moved back to hers, and I gave her another kiss before I pulled away.

She was winded by my affection, like always. Her hands rested against my chest, and she wore that sexy look in her eyes, the same expression she showed when she was on her back and her legs were wide apart. "What brings you here?"

"You know how you can't sleep when I'm at work?"

She ran her hands down my chest, pressing through the thin fabric of my t-shirt so she could feel my abs. "Yes."

"Well, I can't do anything while you're at work."

"Well, that's not good because I need to make money."

"No, you don't." I continued to stand against her, not caring if a customer walked through the door. "You're the richest woman in this country—because I'm the richest man in this city."

The corner of her mouth rose in a smile. "Your money isn't my money, Bosco. I've never wanted it, and I still don't. I like my profits. It's not a fortune by any means, but it's mine. I can afford a nice apartment, a car payment, food, and I can pay back my father for opening my shop in the first place."

"You're paying him back?" I asked in surprise.

"He didn't want me to, but I insisted. If this

were Carter, he would expect to be reimbursed because it's part of a life lesson. But since I'm a girl…he goes so easy on me. That's not what I wanted. I pointed that out to him, reminded him it was sexist, so he caved. My father took care of me for eighteen years. He did his job. Now it's my time to take care of myself."

I admired her for her stubbornness. Most women wouldn't have cared to pay him back, and I didn't even want her to pay him back. But when she made that argument, I couldn't help but respect her. "You're so hot, you know that?" My fingers touched her neck under her curtain of hair.

"Hot?" she asked, being playful.

"You've got balls. I like that."

She chuckled. "You should really think about what you just said…"

I pressed my forehead to hers and chuckled. "You know what I mean."

Her hands rested in the crook of my arms, and she continued to show off her pretty smile. "As much as I'm enjoying you being here, I should get back to work. I don't distract you at the casino."

"That's all you ever do," I corrected.

She pulled away from me, keeping her hips away from my hard dick. "I'll see you at home later."

"Actually, I was headed to the cemetery. Wanted to buy some flowers for my mom." She'd been gone for many years, but I made sure I didn't forget her. She was too important to my life to fade away like an old memory.

Carmen looked at me, her face immediately hardening in pain. "Oh…of course. Let me make something special for her." She moved to the counter and pulled on her gloves. She picked a few blue flowers, mixed them in with some white lilies, and added a few pink roses. "How about this?"

"Lovely."

She wrapped them up for me.

I pulled the cash from my wallet.

She pushed my arm down. "A gift from me to her."

Being the stubborn man that I was, I wanted to pay her. I made millions of dollars every single day. I didn't want to take a penny from her. But her gesture was sweet, and I didn't want to ruin that with my testosterone-fueled bullshit. "Thank you." I put my wallet away and took the flowers. "I know you're working right now, but it would mean a lot if you came with me." I'd never taken someone to the cemetery with me. Even Ronan and I went at separate times.

If she had to stay at the shop, I wouldn't be angry with her, but the request didn't seem to disappoint her. "I would love to. Just let me lock up."

"My mother is in Siena, so it's a bit of a drive."

"Then I'll just close up for good." She went behind the counter and put all her work tools away before she grabbed her things.

I kept a stoic expression, but the gesture pulled at

my heartstrings. It didn't seem like she was coming just because I asked. It seemed like she wanted to come. She wanted to be there for me.

I DROVE THE BUGATTI INTO THE COUNTRYSIDE, heading to Siena, which was a short distance away. My men followed behind at a distance, giving me the peace and quiet I craved during times like these.

"I've never seen you drive a car before." She sat in the passenger seat with the flowers in her lap.

"I have at least a dozen of them in the garage."

"Why do you have them if you never drive?"

I shrugged. "I guess they're high-powered trophies."

"My brother likes Bugattis. Says it's the one competitor he actually respects."

"I have a few of his cars in the garage, actually." I liked the sleek design on the outside and the way he didn't compromise on power while making his engines environmentally friendly.

"He'd be flattered."

I entered the city then took the road to the cemetery. It was sunny but cool. The cemetery was deserted, and we seemed to be the only visitors that afternoon. I parked the car a distance away then killed the engine. "It's her birthday today."

"Oh…" She gave me a sad smile then placed her hand on mine. "How old would she have been?"

"Fifty-seven."

She sighed with sadness. "That's so young…"

"I know." I looked straight ahead with her hand in mine, not afraid to show my emotion in front of her. My mother's death still filled me with so much pain. I'd never been dependent on anyone for anything, but my mother was different. I missed her because I loved her, not just because of everything she did for me. "It's not fair. I still struggle with it."

"It's understandable. If I lost my parents…I would never get over it. They could be a hundred, and I would still think it was too soon." She squeezed my hand again.

Her father would probably live to be a hundred just so he could look after her.

We left the car and walked to the plot Ronan and I had bought for her. It had a large tombstone decorated with an angel. She had extra space around her area, a private plot so I could visit her without other people around.

Carmen stood at my side then placed the flowers against the tombstone, the arrangement handmade for my mother. She came back to me then hooked her arm through mine, her face leaning against my shoulder. "I'm so sorry, babe."

Despite my misery, I loved hearing her call me that. I loved hearing the affection in her voice as well as the love. I loved having this woman on my arm, carrying the weight for me so I didn't have to carry it alone. The bad shit in life seemed a lot more bearable when I had someone to share it with. I'd decided I would be alone for the rest of my life, focused on making money and maintaining my power. But now that I had something more important than all of that, those things didn't matter anymore. Money and security didn't console me during my grief.

It was Carmen.

We stood there together for at least fifteen minutes, staring down at my mother's grave. Her tombstone showed my name as well as my brother's. We were the two people who survived her since she didn't have any other family.

Footsteps sounded behind us, and I turned to see who was approaching.

It was Ronan, with his own handful of flowers. "Sorry to interrupt…" He placed his flowers beside mine before he stood up again.

Carmen left my side and hugged him, squeezing him around the waist as she rested her head against his chest.

He hugged her back before he kissed her on the forehead.

I didn't mind the affection, knowing my brother looked at her like a sister.

He came to me next and sighed. "I think Mom would be happy to see us together on her birthday."

"I think so too." I wrapped my arm around his

shoulder and stood at his side, looking down at our mother's gravesite.

Carmen came back into my side and hugged my waist.

The three of us stood together at my mother's grave, and with both of them there, it was the first time visiting my mother wasn't brutally painful.

———

THE SECOND WE WERE HOME, I HAD CARMEN ON HER back, her naked body pressed against the sheets with her head on the pillow. My arms were pinned behind her knees, and I was inside her instantly, relieved the second her wet pussy was wrapped around my length. When we were naked and combined, nothing else in the outside world mattered. It was just the two of us.

There was no such thing as pain.

I moved between my woman's legs and cherished the pussy I was obsessed with. No other woman had ever felt this good, had ever motivated me to take the condom off and commit to her. They were all the same. Carmen was the only one who was different.

She was as beautiful as she was smart. She was as sassy as she was bold. She was perfect in every single way.

The perfect woman.

I took my time, slowly rocking into her and feeling my toes arch in pleasure. There was nowhere else I'd rather be than nine inches deep inside this cunt. A high-stakes poker game wasn't nearly as exciting, nor a cigar or the smoothest scotch in the world.

Nothing could compare to Carmen.

I moved deep and hard between her legs, feeling the stickiness develop between our bodies. If I pulled my dick out, there would be a line of drool between us because her pussy was so wet and my dick was so hard. "Tell me you love me." I held my weight on my arms as my hips pressed deep into her body, my cock moving all the way until only my balls were left in the cold. I pulled back and prepared to slam into her again, claiming her over and over.

Her lips were open in the sexiest way, and her eyes were bright with desire. "I love you…"

I shoved myself inside her harder. "Again."

Her tits shook with my momentum. "I love you." She bit her lip when the words were out of her mouth, like saying them out loud turned her on.

"Again." I could get off on that confession so easily, even though I was demanding her to say those words out loud.

"I love you, babe." She dug her nails into my ass and pulled me inside her, my big dick hitting her as deep as possible. She squeezed my girth as she exploded, sheathing my cock with her come and tightness.

Now my head was in the clouds, and I couldn't think clearly. I thrust into her hard and fast, going from slow and steady to wild and rough. I pounded her ass into the bed and stretched out her pussy, claiming it as mine. Then I filled her slit with my come, making my nightly deposit so it would sit inside her until morning. "Fuck…" I was balls deep, making sure she got every single drop until my cock was absolutely finished.

She moved her fingers into my hair and clutched. "Now say you love me." Her legs were still stretched apart because I was deep inside her. Her wetness soaked into my length, and now my come was mixed with hers.

I kissed her perfect tits then her neck. "I love you, Beautiful. With all my heart."

***

I STOPPED BY THE FLOWER SHOP A FEW DAYS LATER, TO see if she wanted to get lunch. When I walked inside, she was doing the same thing she always did, creating beautiful arrangements to put on display in the window. She knew her way around a pair of shears and moved quickly to make the perfect bouquets for people to take home.

I walked around the shop, impressed by her work ethic but also disappointed she didn't stay home all day with me. It would be nice if we had the whole day together before I went to work, but sometimes I only saw her for a few hours before I went to the casino.

She turned to me when she realized she wasn't alone. Instead of giving me a generic greeting, she smiled. "You've been stopping by a lot lately." She took off her thick gloves and rose on her tiptoes to give me a kiss.

"I miss you." My hand squeezed the fabric of her sweater against her lower back as I pulled her in close.

"Well, you can miss me at home."

"No. My dick prefers your pussy over my hand." I never jerked off anymore, even when she was gone all day. I preferred one of her beautiful holes to my palm. There was no amount of lube I could squirt into my hand that would compare to her wetness.

"What a compliment," she said with a chuckle.

"And I miss everything else about you too." My fingers moved under her chin so I could get a good look at her face. "From those beautiful eyes, to that smart mouth, and your even more gorgeous soul." I'd never said anything romantic in my life, but with her, everything came pouring out. It was easy with Carmen, natural.

Her eyes glanced down as her cheeks reddened. "Who knew Bosco Roth could be so sweet…"

"Who knew Bosco Roth could fall head over heels for a woman?" My fingers pulled her hair from her face. "But he has. And that's never going to change." Even if she left me, I would never stop loving her. I would always dream of her, wish she were mine.

"Are you here to get into my pants?" she whispered. "Because it worked."

"Actually, I wanted to take you to lunch."

"Wow, we've never done that before."

"And we don't need to clear out the restaurant."

"Even better," she said with a laugh. "But unfortunately, I already have plans. I'm going out with Vanessa."

Since both women worked right in town, they spent a lot of time together. "How about I come along? I would love to meet your best friend."

All playfulness evaporated at the question. "Uh…I don't know if that's a good idea."

"Griffin knows about us. It's not like there's anything to hide at this point." In actuality, her father and uncle knew as well. There were no secrets left to reveal. All they were waiting for was the moment she decided what she wanted—if she wanted to be with me or not.

"It's not that…"

"Then what?" I asked. "You've gotten to know Ronan. I should get to know her."

"Not the same thing," she said. "And I'm not sure if Griffin would be okay with that. He, you know…he doesn't…"

"Like me." I smiled, indifferent to his opinion. "I know how he feels about me. And you know I would never do anything to any member of your family—as I've promised. Even if I didn't, I'm not gonna hurt some pregnant woman—even if she's a smartass like you."

"Oh, she is," Carmen blurted. "Big time."

"Even better. I like Barsetti women."

She was still uneasy.

"Is it really that big of a deal? Could we just try and see what happens?" I tried not to be offended, especially since I'd threatened her family a few times in the past.

"Why do you want to have lunch with my cousin so bad?"

"I don't. It would just be easier if I could tag along." And if Vanessa liked me, she could vouch for me with Bones. I was putting all my chips into one pile, hoping that my bet was right and Carmen would stay with me. It would be nice to have someone besides Carmen in my corner.

Carmen finally agreed to it. "Alright. I guess we can try…"

———

WE WENT TO A BISTRO A FEW BLOCKS AWAY, AND Vanessa was already there. Wearing a gray sweater that was loose on her arms and with her hair pulled back, she reminded me of her father, Crow. They both had the same olive skin and green eyes. Carmen looked a little different from her father, inherited more of her mother's traits.

Vanessa looked at me then turned away. But then she did a double take, her eyes snapping wide open in shock. She turned to Carmen, her eyes narrowing like she couldn't believe what she was looking at.

This should be fun.

Carmen arrived at the table first. "Hey, so—"

"Oh my god, is that him?" Vanessa stood up and completely ignored me, not caring that I could overhear her since she was talking pretty loudly.

"Uh, yeah," Carmen said. "I—"

Vanessa waved her closer so they could talk in semi-private, but her voice was so expressive that their conversation was still audible. "Jesus Christ, he's gorgeous."

I tried not to grin.

"I know," Carmen whispered. "I told you that."

"Well, you should have emphasized a little more," Vanessa hissed back. "And secondly, why the hell did you bring him here?"

"I thought we could all have lunch together."

"Are you crazy?" There was really no point for them to speak in private because I could hear every word. Vanessa was too excited, scared, and freaked out to speak at a whisper. "If Griffin finds out about this, he's gonna go ballistic. He was already ballistic, but now he's psychotic with his son inside my belly."

"I know, but he wanted to get to know you," Carmen said back.

"My husband hates him," Vanessa whispered but not low enough. "And since I'm married to him, I have to take his side."

"But I'm your cousin," Carmen reminded her. "And when everyone hated Griffin and refused to give him a chance, I saw past that and gave him a chance. I trusted your instincts and saw the way he loved you. I didn't care what my parents said about him or how your parents felt about him. I gave him a clean slate. I would hope you would do the same for me…"

Guilt spread across Vanessa's face once she heard her cousin's speech. She didn't have a single argument against it because there was nothing she could say to that.

I loved the way Carmen stood up for me.

Vanessa finally gave a nod. "You're right…"

"Thank you," Carmen said.

Vanessa sighed then walked up to me. "I'm sorry about that. I just—"

"Please, don't." I extended my hand. "Bosco. It's a pleasure to meet you, Vanessa."

Vanessa forced a smile as she shook my hand. "You too."

"And congratulations on your son." I gave her a playful smile, letting her know I overheard every single word they'd exchanged.

Her hand went over her stomach. "Thank you…"

We sat together at the table, and I pulled Carmen's chair out for her, not to put on a show, but because I already treated her like a queen. My hand rested on the back of her chair, and I looked at the menu.

It was tense at first, the silence louder than the sounds of people in the restaurant. Vanessa stared at Carmen with the same look of discomfort on her face, and Carmen was still as a statue. Neither one of them looked at the menu.

"Beautiful, what are you getting?" I asked, trying to lighten the sour mood.

"I always get the ravioli." She gave an explanation for why she didn't look at her menu.

"You get the same thing as well?" I asked Vanessa.

"Lasagna," Vanessa said. "And fries. That's what he's been craving."

"There are worse things," Carmen said. "Like pickles dipped in peanut butter."

Vanessa chuckled. "Yeah, I guess so. Thank goodness he likes fried potatoes. I already liked those anyway."

"What are you getting, babe?" Carmen asked me.

I tried not to smile at the nickname. "A salad."

She shot me a venomous glare.

I chuckled. "Kidding. I'm getting the lunch special."

Carmen withdrew her claws. "Good."

"What's that about?" Vanessa asked.

"Bosco only eats fish, vegetables, and boring garbage all the time." Carmen rolled her eyes. "It's torture living with him sometimes. The food is bad, but the sex is good…so it balances out."

I wanted to stick out my chest with pride at that last part. "I don't eat garbage, just to clarify."

"I beg to differ," Carmen said.

"What qualifies as garbage?" Vanessa asked, amused by the conversation.

"Let me put it this way," Carmen said. "He never eats carbs."

Vanessa looked disturbed, like that was the worst news she could have ever received. "Ugh, I'm so sorry, Carmen."

"I know," she said with a sigh.

"Griffin is like that too," Vanessa said. "I'll eat a bowl of cereal or mac and cheese that comes in a box just so I'll survive."

Carmen shook her head. "So shitty."

My hand moved to the center of her back, touching her lightly. The ends of her strands wrapped around my fingers, and I gently played with them.

"So, how's the baby?" Carmen asked. "Anything new?"

"Well…" Vanessa rubbed her stomach. "I picked out a name and asked Griffin if it was okay…and he said yes."

"Ooh…what is it?" Carmen asked.

She took a deep breath before she said the name out loud. "Crow."

"Aww." Carmen covered her mouth with her hands, her eyes immediately watering. "That is so sweet. He's gonna love that. You're gonna make that stern and hard man succumb to tears."

"I know," Vanessa said. "He named me after his sister…and I wanted to name my son after someone great. The name came to me a long time ago. I wasn't sure if Griffin would approve, but he did right away."

"Because that man loves you."

I'd only met Crow once, and he was so quiet and inherently hostile it was hard to imagine him being tender and sweet like his daughter. But he was probably like Cane, only showing affection when there was no one else around. Now I understand just how close Carmen was to her family.

And how steep my odds were.

"I know he does," Vanessa said. "But I think he likes the name too, honestly. He's become so close to my father working with him every day. They have their own relationship now that has nothing to do with me."

"They've come a long way," Carmen said. "I remember when my father punched him…and Griffin just took it."

"Yeah, he had to deal with a lot," Vanessa said in agreement, her eyes drifting to mine. "So…I feel like I know everything about you. It's honestly all Carmen and I ever talk about."

"I hope some good things are said…once in a while." I was sure Vanessa had been whispering in Carmen's ear to leave me. Maybe getting to know me would change her mind.

"Yes," Carmen said. "Not a lot. But sometimes."

I loved her playfulness, so I moved my hand to the back of her neck and gently rubbed it, forgetting about Vanessa for a second and just focusing on Carmen. She brought a light to my life I hadn't realized I needed until now. I'd been living in eternal darkness for so long that I just got used to it. But now that I'd seen the light, I never wanted to go back again.

Vanessa watched us together. "You treating my girl right?"

"Yes. Always." I turned my gaze back to her. "This woman has a lot of power over me. I'm only admitting it because she's figured it out by now. I wasn't the kind of man I should have been in the beginning, but sometimes a man needs to meet the right woman to figure out who he wants to be. And I also think good guys are overrated. Barsetti women aren't looking for an average man with an average life. They're looking for rough and hard men like their fathers and brothers." I shrugged. "It doesn't surprise me."

Carmen and Vanessa looked at each other, like they'd never noticed the trend before.

Now that I'd met Crow and Cane in person, it was obvious to me right away. These women were strong and fearless because of their fathers, so they wanted men who were just as brave, powerful, and courageous. They wouldn't find that in an average man. Not possible.

"So do you have any hobbies?" Vanessa asked, trying to ask me something unrelated to my profession and her obvious disapproval of my past behavior.

"Carmen," I said honestly. "She's all I really think about. I have one younger brother whom I'm close to. We run the casino together. My mother passed away from cancer five years ago, so he's the only family I have left. The rest of my life revolves around work, maintaining membership dues, and keeping the peace within the casino. I've been managing it for ten years now with rare hiccups."

"I'm sorry about your mom," Vanessa said. "I'm grateful I haven't lost a parent yet. I'll never be the same once that day comes and goes."

"Me neither." Carmen placed her hand on mine under the table.

Her affection was nice.

Vanessa looked past us, and her eyes widened in horror. "Griffin."

He was on me with a speed that contradicted his size. He grabbed me by the neck then punched me so hard I careened into the wall.

Everyone in the restaurant turned at the commotion, but no one intervened, probably because Griffin was unstoppable.

My men would move in any second now.

"Griffin!" Vanessa ran around the table and tried to grab his arm.

Carmen moved in the way, placing her body in front of mine.

It took me a second to recover because I wasn't expecting to be hit like that out of nowhere. "Carmen, move." I got to my feet and gently pushed her out of the way. "I don't want you to get hurt."

Griffin's nostrils flared like a bull, and all his muscles bulged with enough thickness to stop a piercing bullet.

"Stay the fuck away from my wife. You fucking piece of shit." He grabbed me by the throat and bashed my head into the wall.

"Stop it!" Carmen shoved him as hard as she could.

I was powerless to do anything, since I promised Carmen I would never hurt her family. I just had to take it.

My men came in with their weapons drawn. The barrels were pointed right at Griffin's head, and they were ready to pull the trigger. "Stand down. Leave." I leaned against the wall, barely able to stand because my head was throbbing from hitting the wall twice. "Leave him be…"

They filed out, listening to my order because they knew what would happen if they didn't.

Carmen moved in front of me again, pressing her back into my chest so Griffin would have to hit her if he wanted to strike me again. "What the hell is wrong with you?"

Griffin's face was tomato red with rage. He raised his muscular arm and pointed his finger in my face. "My wife is off-limits. I told you to stay the fuck away from her. Come near my wife or my son, and I'll fucking kill you next time."

"Griffin, he wasn't hurting me," Vanessa said. "We were just having lunch—"

"Shut up." He didn't look at her as he silenced her. "I'll deal with you later."

Vanessa's rage was even more potent than his. Her

hands moved to her hips as she seemed to grow twice in size. She stared at the side of her husband's face, her eyes filled with wrath and threat. "Excuse me?"

Griffin ignored her. "I'm not kidding, Bosco. I have no control over Carmen's life. But I don't want you anywhere near my wife without me standing there. Do it again, and I'll put you in the ground. I don't give a shit if your dogs come after me and put me in the ground with you."

Despite my migraine, I admired his commitment.

"Griffin." Carmen's voice had softened, filling with heavy disappointment. "I was the only one who took your side when it mattered most. I believed in you when no one else did. When my father hit you, I told him off and called him an asshole. I've always stood up for you because I knew you loved Vanessa. This is how you repay me?"

Griffin's eyes moved to her face. Despite his anger, he softened slightly—for her. "It's not the same."

"It is the same. Griffin, this is the man I love. He loves me. I understand if you don't like him, but at least be civil. Don't storm in here and throw him against the wall. The only reason he's not fighting back is because he promised me he would never hurt any of you. He kept his promise and made sure you didn't get shot. So now it's your turn to make that promise to me." She poked her finger in his chest. "Don't touch Bosco ever again."

"Vanessa—"

"He's not gonna hurt Vanessa," she hissed. "We were talking about food, your son, and Bosco's mom before you stormed in here like some kind of lunatic. Everything was fine until you ruined it. Did it seem like Vanessa was in trouble?"

He stared at her without blinking, his blue eyes bright like mine. "When it comes to my wife and son, I don't take chances. Vanessa has been taken from me before, and I can't let that happen again, not when we have a little one joining us soon. I'm sorry that I overreacted, but my position still stands. I don't want him around her unless I'm right there. I'm the shield that protects both of them, and I don't want her near this asshole unprotected. You know I love you, Carmen. You make a valid point about what you did for me before. I will try because it's important to you. But I'm not gonna change my mind about that last part. Accept that compromise because that's the best you'll get from me." He stepped back and turned to Vanessa.

But she was just as pissed as before. "Oh, are you ready to deal with me now?" Her hands were still on her hips, her attitude in full force. "Put your wife in her place? Tell her how to behave?" Her wrath was somehow worse than Griffin's.

Carmen turned to me next and examined me. "Babe, are you okay?"

The pain was strong, but nothing was broken. "I've lived through worse. I'll be fine." I straightened, ignoring the pain in my skull and standing tall like the man I was.

"I'm so sorry," Carmen whispered as she cupped my face, her eyes filled with pain.

"Don't apologize, Beautiful." I kissed her forehead. "I'm fine."

"You kept your promise to me…"

I kept my promise to her more than she realized. "I don't break my promises."

Griffin turned back to me, still angry any time he looked at me. He wasn't going to apologize and I wouldn't expect him to, but there was a look in his eyes, an expression that wasn't clear. "You love her?"

"You think I would have called off my men if I didn't?" We both knew I had enough power to do whatever I pleased. If Carmen were just my prisoner, I would go ahead and kill him to make my life easier. If I didn't give a damn, I would have killed her father and uncle too. "You think I would be having lunch with Carmen and your wife if I weren't trying to…" I didn't finish the sentence, not wanting to sound like a pussy. "You can do whatever the hell you want to me, Griffin. I promised Carmen I would never hurt any of you. So if you beat me to within an inch of my life, I still won't fight back. I'll kill a man with my bare hands, but I'll also sacrifice my life if that's what Carmen wants. You must not love her as much as I do because you can't keep your shit together."

Griffin didn't react to my words, his eyes turning to Carmen. "And you love him?"

Carmen nodded. "Yes."

He closed his eyes for a moment, like he was disappointed with the news. "Alright. Then I'll behave from now on—as long as you do as I ask. We have a deal?"

I nodded. "Fine." I was a little annoyed that I'd just proved I would never hurt any of them, but that still wasn't enough for Griffin. If I'd wanted to hurt his wife that much, I would have let my men shoot him so he would be out of the way. He also knew I was an honest man, and that was something he already respected about me.

Griffin turned to Vanessa. "Baby, let's go."

Judging by the way she crossed her arms over her chest and glared at him, that wasn't happening. "No. You're leaving. You're going back to wherever the hell you came from. And maybe tonight when I get off work…I might come home."

Carmen placed the ice against the back of my head to help the swelling go down.

"Beautiful, I told you I'm fine."

"Well, I'm looking at the back of your head, and it's not fine." She sat behind me against the couch, her legs spread around me. She pressed the towel against the back of my head for long stretches of time before she pulled away to let my skin warm up again. "A lot of swelling. Maybe you should see a doctor."

Doctors were for pussies. "I'm fine." I would say it as many times as I had to.

She kept cycling the bag against my head before she pulled it away, giving my skull a chance to thaw out once more. "God, I'm so sorry… I didn't even know Griffin was there until you were against the wall."

"Don't apologize for his actions." I was the one who'd wanted to have lunch with Vanessa. If I was really that worried about Griffin, I could have avoided it. It was entirely my fault. I didn't have any regrets since I'd made some progress with Carmen. Listening to her confess her love for me to Griffin made it all worth it. "He did what he had to do. Let it go."

"He did not have to throw you against a wall."

"Beautiful." I silenced her with her name. "That's how men communicate. Don't worry about it."

"But you were powerless to do anything about it."

"That's what you asked for, right?" I said quietly. Her father and uncle came into my casino and made demands no one else could pull off. Anyone else would have been thrown into the ring for that kind of disrespect. Because of their halo of safety Carmen provided for them, they could have done anything they wanted and gotten away with it. "Maybe Griffin will take me more seriously now."

"I don't know…he's stubborn. I am disappointed in him for being so callous. When he first came around, I defended him to everyone. I treated him like a human being even though everyone said he was dangerous. I ignored his past and focused on his present. I wish he would do the same for me…"

"In his defense, you aren't being fair. His wife being there was the problem. And men can't see straight when it comes to their women."

"He still went overboard. I don't even know how he figured out you were there."

"If he's anything like me, he keeps tabs on Vanessa." I would do the same thing, whether Carmen was pregnant or not. I reached behind me and grabbed the bag of ice out of her hands. "Stop being my nurse."

"I like taking care of you." She wrapped her arms around my waist and kissed my shoulders, her soft lips grazing over the hot skin. "I feel so terrible, babe. It breaks my heart seeing you get hurt."

It broke my heart too. "I'm not hurt." I moved away from her embrace and turned around, showing her I was fine with my steady gaze. I was man enough to handle anything Griffin did to me. After a few days, the migraine would disappear, and I would be as good as new. It wasn't in my nature to show any kind of weakness. Even in the final weeks of my mother's life, she never showed the pain she was enduring. She continued to wear a smile and treasure her final moments with us. She was a badass and didn't let the cancer defeat her, even at the very end.

I could handle a fucking migraine.

She tilted her head as she looked at me, the disappointment in her gaze. "You're the kind of man that refuses to show your suffering, huh?"

"I'm not suffering."

She smiled. "There's my answer. My father is the same way. Drives my mother crazy."

Because that was how men should be.

"I feel responsible for this, so I feel terrible…" She rubbed my thigh. "I wish there was something I could do to make you feel better."

"Well, there's always something you can do…"

The corner of her mouth rose in a smile. "Is that all you ever think about?"

"Yes." I blurted out my answer without thinking twice about it. "Always."

"Alright." She guided my back against the couch then straddled my hips. "What can I do to make it up to you?" She pushed down the front of my sweatpants so my hardening cock would appear.

She had nothing to make up for because it wasn't her fault, but I wouldn't tell her that. "So many things I would like…" My fingers wrapped around her neck, feeling her soft pulse under my touch. It was quickly accelerating, either because she was scared or a little bit nervous. I brushed my thumb along her bottom lip as I stared at it, noticing the plumpness while feeling the softness. My eyes moved to her tits next, studying them in the sweater she still wore. I could see the outline of her curves, the swell of her perfect rack.

Now that my mind was on sex, my migraine was forgotten.

"Have you decided?" She wrapped her fingers around my hard dick and swiped her thumb over the head, catching the drop that had formed at the tip. The stickiness stretched between her thumb and her finger.

I watched her hand get messy from the arousal that poured out of my dick, and I preferred to see that stickiness stretch from her tongue to my tip. "A five-star blow job and a tit-fuck." I would get to sit back and watch her please me, cashing in on the reward that I'd earned that afternoon.

She pulled her sweater over her head and unclasped her bra, revealing her perfect tits. "Your wish is my command."

I inhaled a deep breath through my clenched teeth, loving that line coming out of her pretty mouth.

5

VANESSA

I WAS PISSED at Griffin for many reasons.

I didn't even know where to begin.

In the past eighteen months, there had been a lot of growth. He wasn't the barbaric animal who barked out orders anymore. He was laid-back, calm, and civil. But all that went out the window, and he treated me like some kind of slave.

He'll deal with me later?

Uh, I don't think so.

I took a cab to my gallery then entered our apartment above the shop. We hadn't been there much since we moved out to Tuscany. All the furniture was still there because the place was furnished when Griffin bought it. I decided to stay there for the night since the idea of sleeping beside my husband didn't sound appealing.

That was a first.

He didn't call me or try to track me down.

That could only mean he knew exactly where I was. He probably never let me out of his sight once I stormed out.

There were some old protein bars in the cabinet so I knew I would be able to hold out until morning, even when the baby was so hungry. But I could also order pizza if he really became rambunctious.

I spent the rest of the day there and deep into the night.

Griffin still didn't call me.

I sat on the couch and stared at the front door, suspecting he was right outside. Maybe he was sitting in his truck at the curb the way he used to at my old apartment in Milan. As if I could feel his presence through the solid wall, I knew he was outside somewhere. He would never go home and leave me here.

I moved to the front door and looked out the peephole, suspecting I'd see his truck at the curb. But there was nothing to see.

The apartment was warm because a fire was burning, and the heater brought warmth to the living room, but I kept my sweater on because I was focused on keeping my son warm all the time. I opened the door, not sure what I expected to find.

Sitting outside in the middle of the freezing cold was Griffin. He was on the top step that led to the apartment, wearing nothing but a t-shirt and jeans. Vapor escaped his nostrils, but he didn't shake despite the cold. He was immune to it, thriving in it just as he did the night we met. He didn't turn around to look at me.

I leaned against the doorway. "Griffin."

He brought his hands together and slowly rubbed his palms across one another. "I'm not gonna leave, so save it." His deep voice was menacing, warning me he didn't want to have an argument about this. He wasn't going to leave me alone no matter how much I fought it, so I might as well save my energy as well as my time. "Be angry all you want. I won't abandon my duty. I'll sit out here all night because it's where I belong— protecting you." Like a watchdog, he stared out to the street where a single streetlamp stood. It was the only light visible between the two buildings.

My anger hadn't diminished, but I wasn't a psychopath who would leave my husband sitting outside when the temperatures were close to freezing. "Come in." I left the door open and walked back inside. There was an extra blanket in the basket so I tossed it on the couch. I grabbed an extra pillow from the bedroom and returned to the living room to set it down.

Griffin stood in front of the fire, staring at the couch like he had no idea what it was. He looked at it for nearly a full minute before he lifted his gaze to look at me. "No."

"Yes." I turned around and headed down the hall-way. "Good night."

His heavy footsteps followed me instantly.

I turned around. "I'm serious." I looked up into his handsome face, immune to his charm because I was still livid with him.

"I'm not sleeping on the couch."

"You bet your ass, you are." I gave him a glare full of warning before I stepped inside the bedroom.

He followed me anyway.

"Griffin!"

He stripped off his shirt then moved to his jeans, ignoring me.

"Fine. Then I'll sleep on the couch." I turned around to march off.

He grabbed me by both arms and yanked me into his chest, restraining me so I couldn't go anywhere. "You married me. You promised yourself to me for the rest of your life. So for better or worse, we're sleeping in the same fucking bed. Be pissed at me all you want. It's not gonna change anything."

"There you go again." I twisted out of his grasp. "Bossing me around like you own me."

His eyes narrowed. "I do own you."

My hand was shaking because I wanted to slap him.

"And you own me." He grabbed both of my wrists, probably because he knew I was about to strike him. "I need to be there for anything, baby. I need to take care of you and our son. I'm sleeping right beside you so I can wait on you hand and foot. Get over it." He released me and walked back to the bed.

"And that's it?" I asked incredulously. "You aren't even going to apologize?"

He dropped the rest of his clothes, stripping down to his nakedness even though we wouldn't be having sex tonight. He pulled back the sheets and got into bed. "I don't apologize unless I mean it. So, no, don't expect one."

I actually growled under my breath because I was so pissed off. "Fuck you, Griffin." I marched back down the hallway into the living room. I expected my husband to apologize to me for crossing the line and telling me to shut up. I expected some kind of remorse and a vow never to repeat those mistakes. But he was still behaving like an asshole, and it was the first time I genuinely didn't want to be around him.

His footsteps sounded a moment later. "Get your ass in there."

"Shut up," I hissed. "Just leave me alone, Griffin. I'm serious." I grabbed the pillow and blanket so I could get comfortable near the fire.

He stood there with his arms tensing by his sides, his soft but enormous dick hanging between his legs. His eyes were wide with rage, and it seemed like he wanted to grab me by both arms and throw me around.

"I've never been so disappointed in you." I lay down and pulled the blanket to my shoulder before I stared at the fire. I didn't want to look at him right then. I wanted nothing to do with him.

He continued to stand there like he didn't know

what else to do. Then he moved to the other couch and got as comfortable as possible, his feet hanging over the edge because he was too big for the piece of furniture. "Go to bed. I'll stay here." He brought the conversation to a close by turning silent.

I couldn't believe that this was really happening, that Griffin really didn't think he owed me an apology. I left my stuff behind and walked into the bedroom, making sure to slam the door as hard as I could just so he would hear the echo.

I got into bed, but I couldn't sleep, either because I was too pissed off or because my husband wasn't beside me.

Maybe it was both.

GRIFFIN WAS SITTING ON THE COUCH WHEN I WOKE up the next morning. He'd just finished his coffee, and he was on his phone, wearing the clothes he was wearing yesterday. He didn't look up to greet me, ignoring me the way I ignored him.

I grabbed my purse off the table along with my phone and headed to the door.

"Vanessa." Griffin's deep voice made me stop in my tracks.

I slowly turned around, looking him in the eye while mirroring his same look of fury. "Griffin."

He rose to his feet and placed his phone in his

pocket. "You put yourself in danger, and that's unacceptable."

"Put myself in danger?" I asked incredulously, having no idea what he was talking about.

"Don't play stupid," he hissed.

"I had no idea he was going to be there until he walked in the door. It's not like I planned it—"

"But you didn't call me. You should have fucking called me." He slammed his hand into his chest hard, turning barbaric. "It's my job to protect you, and we both know I take my job fucking seriously. And that's my son in there." He placed his hand against my stomach, being delicate despite the way he'd just slammed his hand into his body. "How dare you bring him around the biggest crime lord in the damn country? That's unforgivable, Vanessa."

"You really think Carmen would bring him around if he was ever going to hurt me?"

"Well, she's an idiot for getting involved with him in the first place."

"Am I an idiot for getting involved with you?" I countered.

That shut him up.

"You're overreacting. Bosco was nothing but polite, friendly, and kind. He didn't exhibit any of the traits you've credited him with. And when you were going ape-shit crazy on him, he didn't fight back. He called off his dogs. He's proven he's not a threat to us, Griffin. So how dare you get so angry with me?"

"Because." He ground his jaw tightly. "You had no idea what his plan was. You should have called me." He slammed his hand into his chest like an animal once more. "You are my wife and my responsibility. We have a son, and we can't take any chances. You have no idea what I went through when you were taken from me. And if that happened again...but with my son inside you..." He shook his head as his nostrils flared, like he couldn't say any more. "You should have called me. So when you apologize for that, I'll consider apologizing to you."

I'd never seen Griffin behave so arrogantly. I knew he was still pissed off so he couldn't see clearly, but it was still ridiculous. "You're overreacting. If Bosco wanted to hurt any of us, he would have done it already. He loves Carmen, and I can see it written all over his face without him saying it. Maybe he's not Prince Charming, but neither were you. And maybe that's not what Carmen wants. I understand you're paranoid because of the things that have happened in the past, but you need to let that go."

"Let that go?" he asked coldly. His hands shook by his sides like he wanted to slam both of them into his chest and break himself in half. "You were the most important thing to me, and my life wasn't worth living without you. But now that I feel my son kick, hear his heartbeat...I've come to realize that I love him more than I will ever love you. It fucking hurts, Vanessa. I love him so much it kills me. So I can't think straight when it comes to him. If there's any chance of something happening to him, I can't risk it. We're in this together, and you should have talked to me. Don't pretend the thought didn't cross your mind when you saw him walk in that restaurant. Don't fucking lie to me."

I didn't.

He kept up his look of rage, furious with me just as he was at the start of the conversation. "You know where to find me." He walked away from me without saying goodbye. He didn't tell me he loved me or give me a kiss. He turned his back on me, being colder to me than he'd ever been before.

6

GRIFFIN

WHEN I GOT to the winery, I went straight to work in the warehouse. I avoided Crow and Cane because I was so furious I couldn't see straight. I took care of the orders and prepared to ship them out on the shipping truck even though that wasn't exactly in my job description anymore.

The manual labor helped relieve my rage, and we were able to get the truck loaded in a fraction of the time it normally took. When I went back into the warehouse, I calculated how much of the harvest was left before I went over the orders we would need when spring arrived.

It was past noon when Crow stepped into the warehouse.

I didn't want to see him right then. I didn't want to see anyone. I'd considered taking a personal day just to avoid him. Whenever I was angry, my temper exploded like a bomb, and the fallout lasted for weeks.

Crow came to my side, examining my features like he knew something was wrong. "Everything alright, son?"

He called me and Conway by the same name, making me a part of his family in a way I'd never expected. The affectionate term didn't pierce my solid armor. I was too far gone. "I don't want to talk about it."

Crow continued to stand there, sliding his hands into his pockets.

I kept working, doing my best to ignore him. When minutes passed and he stayed, I knew he wasn't going anywhere. "Yes?"

"Whenever there's something bothering Vanessa and Conway, I usually just wait until they tell me what's wrong. I don't ask any questions, but they usually open up to me whenever they're ready. So I'll stand here and wait." He grabbed the order sheet I was working on and scanned through it, checking through all the data I'd just reported.

I was annoyed with Crow for infringing on my space. I'd never had anyone do that before, not even Vanessa. It didn't seem like he was being nosy; he just wanted to help me. I didn't have any other relationship to compare it to, but it seemed like a relationship a father and son would have.

Crow was the closest thing I'd ever had to a father.

"Vanessa and I are going through a hard time." I stared at the crates in front of me and didn't make eye contact with him. It was strange to talk to him about his daughter, but I suspected he already assumed she was the reason I was angry. "She pissed me off, and I'm still pissed off."

"What'd she do?"

"She put herself in danger, and she acts like it's no big deal." I finally ignored the crates and met his gaze. "She had lunch with Bosco and Carmen yesterday. Her bodyguard told me about it, so I hauled ass until I got into Florence and slammed Bosco into a wall. Vanessa was upset with me…and I said some things I shouldn't. But I'm pissed she brushed it off. I'm pissed she didn't call me. I'm pissed she doesn't take this seriously. She's carrying our son. I haven't even met him, and I worry about him all the time."

Crow didn't react as he listened, behaving impartially to the story.

"I haven't apologized because I want an apology from her first. I damaged Bosco pretty badly, but he didn't retaliate. His men came in to shoot me, but he called them off. Said he promised Carmen he would never hurt any of us…and he kept his promise. He probably isn't a threat, but that's not the point."

Crow crossed his arms over his chest and leaned against one of the crates.

"I know what it's like to lose her. I couldn't go

through that again…not with my son too. I wish she understood that, but it doesn't seem like she does."

Crow continued to listen, remaining quiet until I was completely finished. "Pearl did something stupid shortly after we were married. I'll skip the specifics. She basically put herself at risk with a few demons to help someone else…and she did it alone. When I found out about it and confronted her…" He shook his head and rubbed the back of his head. "I did something really terrible. I was just so angry with her for putting herself at risk, especially after everything I did to keep her safe. So…I slapped her. Slapped her hard."

I couldn't hide my surprise, shocked that Crow would do something like that.

"It was over thirty years ago. I haven't done it again because I understood how wrong it was. I didn't want to be that man ever again, regardless of how much she pissed me off. She forgave me…even when I didn't deserve it."

I didn't know what to say. I would never raise my hand to Vanessa, no matter how angry she made me.

"Our women will never understand what it's like to be in our shoes. And frankly, they shouldn't have to. They have their own burdens, their own sacrifices they make for us on a regular basis. I understand why you're upset. You just want Vanessa to be safe. But you're never going to get your point across by pushing her away in the process. When it comes to marriage, there's no such thing as keeping score. Apologize for what you said, then tell her how you feel. I know my daughter. She's so stubborn that she won't listen until she gets the apology she deserves. Unfortunately, that means you need to cave first. It sucks, but your marriage is more important than your sacrifice."

I could tell he'd been married for a long time based on what he said. I slid my hands into my pockets as I considered his words. I was a simple man with simple needs. One of those needs was for Vanessa's safety. If that requirement wasn't met, I was often deranged.

"I hope that was helpful." He clapped my shoulder before he walked out.

7

VANESSA

I SPENT most of the day in a pissed mood.

I wasn't even hungry.

I'd never been so angry with Griffin. If he thought he could talk to me that way and get away with it just because I loved him, that was an idiotic excuse. I wasn't putting up with it. I was the one carrying his son, and I would have to push him out in a few months.

Griffin should be kissing the ground I walked on.

My phone rang, and my father's name appeared on the screen. I knew Griffin would never talk to my father about any of this, so I assumed he was calling about something else. "Hey, Father. How are you?"

"Hey, *tesoro*." His mood was somber, like this wouldn't be a pleasant conversation. He didn't answer my question.

"Everything alright?"

"I just talked to Griffin."

I stilled at the surprise. Griffin wasn't talkative, let alone about our personal relationship. I was surprised he'd confided in my father, even if they were on good terms. "Oh?"

"Yeah. He mentioned what happened."

"And you're calling me because…?" I shouldn't give my father attitude because of Griffin's actions, but it slipped out.

My father let it slide. "Remember how much this man loves you. Remember all the sacrifices he's made for you, made for this family."

Oh no, the guilt trip.

"All he wants is to keep you safe. His heart is in the right place even if his mouth isn't. He's a good man, and you're lucky to have him."

I never thought my father would take Griffin's side on anything. Now it seemed like they were conspiring against me. "Father, I know you're trying to help, but this is between my husband and me. Just because you two are close now doesn't mean you should gang up on me."

"I'm not ganging up on you. He doesn't know about this conversation. I can relate to everything he said because it's exactly how I feel about your mother, about my children. All I want, more than anything in this world, is to keep my family safe. Griffin is the same way. He's not asking for a lot, *tesoro*. All he wants is to protect you. I'm not excusing what he said. But…just keep that in mind. Try to meet him halfway."

I rolled my eyes because he couldn't see me.

"Vanessa." It was like he knew exactly what I just did. "There's no room for stubbornness in a marriage. I learned that the hard way."

AFTER I FINISHED UP AT WORK, I DROVE HOME TO our house in Tuscany. I didn't stay at the apartment again because he would just hunt me down there, and now that we had a beautiful home with a yard, that was where I wanted to be.

Griffin was in the kitchen when I walked inside, working the stove as he made dinner. He didn't look at me when I walked in, but he somehow knew I would come home that night.

I set my purse on the table and hung up my coat on the coatrack. I didn't face him right away because I didn't know what to say. I didn't even know where to start. I finally turned around and walked toward him, my guard up because I didn't know what kind of mood he was in. "Listen…"

He turned off the pans and faced me, cooking with his shirt off even though there was hot oil everywhere and it was fifty degrees outside. He stared at me with an indecipherable expression, his look hard and his jaw tense. His eyes were the only gentle thing about him.

"I did some thinking when I was at work today. I know all you want is to keep us safe…"

His eyes softened immediately, like he'd been hoping I would say those magic words to him.

"I know you love us and—"

He cupped my face and bent his neck down to kiss me. It was an aggressive kiss, but it was soft and loving at the same time. His fingers touched my hair, and he kissed me like he loved me, adored me.

I fell into his kiss, feeling all my anger disappear.

He pulled away and looked at me, the love bright in his eyes. Just like when the clouds passed after a storm, the sun was finally revealed. "Let me take care of you." His hand moved under my shirt to my bare stomach. "Let me protect both of you. Let me lay down my life to keep you safe. That's all I want, baby."

Now I actually felt bad for being so angry with him. His only crime was loving me, loving both of us. "I know…"

He moved to his knees in front of me and kissed my belly before he rested his forehead against it. "Please do as I ask. Even if you think it's ridiculous, just do it for me. We're a team." He lifted his gaze to look at me again. "Let me do my job."

"I will, Griffin. Whatever you want…I'll do it." It went against my stubborn nature to say that, but I forced it out for him.

"Thank you." He kissed my stomach again before he rose to his feet. "And I'm sorry for what I said, baby. I shouldn't have snapped at you like that. I shouldn't have spoken to you that way…it was wrong of me."

I knew he meant what he said, and that was enough for me. "Thank you…"

He stared at me with his hands on my belly, turning back into my husband. He was cold and rough around everyone else, but when it was just the two of us, he was soft in a way no one else ever got to see.

"But we do need to talk about Bosco, Griffin."

"And what is there to say?" He rubbed my stomach with his hands.

"I don't think he's dangerous. I understand why you're worried…but I don't think he's a threat. If you really don't want me to be around him without you, that's fine. But…I do think you're overreacting."

Griffin didn't get angry, probably because I was still willing to give him what he wanted.

"You roughed him up pretty badly, and he didn't do the same to me…and we both know he has the power to do whatever he wants."

Griffin gave a slight nod.

"I also think you should give him a real chance. Maybe he wasn't a good guy before…but he clearly is now. Carmen gave you the benefit of the doubt, and you should do the same for her. That's only fair."

He nodded again. "If they stay together, I'll make a better effort. But until then, I'm not sure how I feel about him. And I don't want my wife and baby around him if I'm not there."

"Alright. Does that mean you'll come to lunch or dinner with us?"

He sighed like that was the most unappealing thing in the world.

"Griffin?" I pressed.

He finally gave an answer. "It looks like I don't have any other choice."

8

CARMEN

THE EVIDENCE of my black eye was finally gone. The blue and purple colors disappeared, the skin returning to its normal shade. It made putting on my makeup much easier, and it didn't make me so self-conscious in public.

I stood in the purple gown Bosco bought for me, a deep royal color that I adored. I did my hair in big curls and wore extra makeup for the evening, detailing my eyes to make them look smoky. I wore my father's necklace and a bracelet Bosco had given me.

Bosco appeared behind me in the mirror, wearing a tuxedo. The material fit him like a second skin, showing his sculpted shoulders and arms. He wore a handsome grin as he came up behind me and presented me with a little black box. "I want you to wear this tonight."

I stared at the little box in his hands and immediately knew it was jewelry. I was already wearing a necklace and a bracelet, so I wasn't sure what else he wanted me to wear. I took it from his hands and popped open the box, revealing two diamond earrings.

Enormous diamond earrings.

"Uh…wow." They caught the light and dazzled like two rainbows. "Jesus, these are huge."

He grabbed my hair and pulled it back behind my shoulders. "Put them on."

"They look too nice to wear. They should be sitting in a safe inside another safe…"

He leaned down and kissed my neck. "Put them on."

I pulled each one out of the box and placed them in my lobes. They possessed a distinct heaviness, but they were also so strikingly beautiful that they pulled my outfit together perfectly. I'd never cared for expensive jewels, but anytime Bosco gave me anything, I loved it.

Bosco put my hair back in place. "Beautiful." He left the bathroom, his dress shoes clapping against the tile. "Ready to go?"

"Yeah. Just let me grab my clutch." I picked up the matching clutch Bosco had given to me, and we left together. We sat in the back seat of the car, and we headed down the road, approaching the opera house where we'd watch our show.

Bosco held my hand in the back seat. The back of his head didn't seem to bother him anymore, and the swelling had gone down. He was as good as new, and as obsessed with me as ever.

"I've never been to the opera before."

"Never?" he asked, his blue eyes shifting to my face. He looked handsome in his tux, his masculine physique filling out the material perfectly, from his broad shoulders to his chiseled jaw and his long legs.

"Never."

"I think you'll enjoy it. If you don't, we can always do something else." The corner of his mouth rose in a smile like he was making a joke.

But I knew it wasn't a joke.

We entered the lobby where other couples were dressed in their finest. Bosco was immediately greeted by a crew that made him feel welcome, treating him like royalty. A few of the other guests looked at him, some with fear and others with respect.

My arm rested in the crook of his, and he guided me up the red-carpeted stairs to a private balcony. The entire box was reserved just for us, so we took the seats in the first row and waited for it to begin.

"You reserved the whole area?" I whispered.

He nodded. "I don't share space with the public."

"I'm surprised you didn't rent out the whole theater, then."

He shrugged. "I know you hate that, so I skipped it."

Both of my eyebrows rose. "You've done that in the past…?"

"Like I said, I don't share my space with the public. Their jealous and envious expressions get old. People ask for my advice or try to pick my brain about the casino. Women offer to suck my dick because they want to be covered in jewels and gowns. It gets tedious, to say the least."

I crossed my legs and rested my arm through his. The lights dimmed, and the curtains opened. The show started, the sound of loud music filling the auditorium. It was a play about falling in love and finding the will to go on when that love was lost forever.

My hand stayed on his, and halfway through the show, I rested my head on his shoulder. When it was just the two of us tucked inside the box, no one else could see us except the actors onstage. That allowed me to be as affectionate as I liked, just as if we were home alone.

His hand lay on my thigh as he watched the play, his warm fingers lightly touching my bare skin. His cologne was powerful, along with his body soap and natural scent. With every breath he took, I could see his muscles flex slightly, making his body rise like a filled balloon.

The show was long, a few hours at least, but sitting with him made me envision our lives together if I stayed. We would do normal things together like this, get dressed up and go to the opera while someone watched the kids. We would still be in love decades later, just the way my parents were. We would be happy, affectionate, and loving.

The thoughts made me weak in the knees and a little afraid. I'd never been able to picture a future with any of the men in my life. I could see the ending right at the beginning. But now I was getting so attached to this man, it was impossible to picture my life without him. We only had a week left together, and on that day, I would leave without looking back.

But now that seemed impossible.

When the lights came up and the curtains closed, applause filled the auditorium.

I sat up straight and clapped, but I was only partially paying attention. All I could focus on was the thoughts that had played through my head during the performance. I couldn't really enjoy it because I kept thinking about the man beside me, the man I leaned on for comfort, the man who decorated me with the most expensive jewels.

"Did you like it?" Bosco turned to me, the look in his eyes painfully handsome.

"Yes…it was beautiful."

"My mom always loved the opera. Ronan and I used to take her."

"You should have brought him along tonight."

He rose to his feet and took me by the hand. "Maybe next time."

WHEN WE RETURNED TO THE PENTHOUSE, I SLIPPED off my heels and left them in the corner of the bedroom, treating his bedroom like it was my own and somewhere I could make a mess. I was tired from the long show and sitting in traffic on the way back.

I was just about to take off my dress when Bosco ordered me not to.

"Leave it on." He undid his bow tie then stripped off his jacket. "On the bed. On your back." He dropped his jacket on the floor, slipped off his shoes, and then removed the rest of his tux, piece by piece.

I did as he asked, getting my purple dress wrinkled in the process.

He stripped down until he was naked then climbed on top of me. "All I could think about was fucking you tonight because you looked so beautiful." He lifted the bottom of my gown and pushed it to my waist. "And now I finally will." He pulled my black thong down my legs then tossed it aside. His eyes took in the area between my legs with arousal before he spread my legs with his knees. He positioned himself on top of me then slid inside, moving through the wetness that had been between my legs since we were in the opera house.

Right from the beginning, he pounded into me, taking me roughly like he was claiming me instead of making love to me. He decorated me in diamonds and designer clothing before he showed me off to the world, using me as another power play for his ego. And then he rewarded himself by fucking me hard in his bed.

I didn't mind in the least. I loved being the object of this man's obsession, loved being the only woman who got to be fucked like this. He could have any other woman, but he only wanted me. He only wanted to be inside me every night, no one else. My hands scratched his back, and I rocked my hips with him. "I love you, Bosco." My heart had been bleeding in that auditorium, thinking about how much I'd fallen for this man. I wanted to do this every night for the rest of my life. I didn't want to replace him with someone else, a good man.

I wanted a dangerous man instead.

I MET VANESSA FOR LUNCH THE NEXT DAY.

"First of all, I have to ask this…" Vanessa looked behind me, expecting to see Bosco come through the door. "Did you bring him along? Because if you did, I have to tell Griffin and—"

"Just me." I'd learned my lesson.

"Oh, thank god," Vanessa said in relief. "I would have to tell Griffin, and it would be a whole ordeal. We just made up, and I don't feel like fighting again."

"I'm so sorry. I feel responsible for all that." If I hadn't brought Bosco with me, none of that would have happened.

"Don't be sorry. Griffin is just a very aggressive and protective man."

"There are worse things."

"Yes…but we can all agree he goes a little overboard."

"I'm glad you two made up," I said. "It seemed pretty tense between you."

"Yeah, we fought for about two days. He even brought my father into it."

"Wait…your father knows about Bosco?"

"No," I said. "I think Griffin just told him a generic story that I was putting myself in danger, because my father didn't ask any specific questions."

I let myself relax. "Phew, thank god."

"I'm really sorry Griffin attacked him like that. I was so embarrassed."

"Bosco was fine. He had a headache for a few days, but it passed." He was a strong man who could take a serious beating without being unsettled. He refused to admit he was in pain. He didn't even take a painkiller for it. He just drank scotch instead. "At least it'll never happen again. I'm sure Griffin won't attack him like that again…right?"

"No. I made sure of that."

I looked at Vanessa before I took a piece of bread out of the basket. "So much for our men getting along…"

"Griffin doesn't get along with anyone, so I wouldn't put much thought into it."

I chuckled. "I guess that's true. So, Griffin doesn't want you anywhere near him?"

"Just not alone. I think he understands Bosco isn't a threat, but he's very paranoid…" She rolled her eyes. "And I can't make him feel bad about that since those men took me to Morocco. He has a right to be paranoid."

"Yeah, it's true. Maybe in time he'll change his mind."

"In time?" she asked, tilting her head slightly sideways. "Does that mean this isn't going to end in a week?"

Our contract only had seven days left, and I was dreading that moment. I didn't want to leave this man, but my gut told me I couldn't stay. "I…I don't know."

Vanessa gave me a sad look. "Carmen, I'm not going to judge you if you want to stay with him. Look who I ended up with. He's the most barbaric man in the world."

"That isn't why," I said with a chuckle. "I just don't know what I want. We went to the opera together the other night, and I was so happy. I pictured our future together, being in love with kids…"

Vanessa kept watching me, her arms resting on the table. "Then stay."

"It's not that simple…"

"If you love him, and he is the only man you've ever loved, then you should fight for it."

"But what kind of future could we have?" I countered. "Griffin won't even let you be around him."

"That will pass," she said firmly. "I saw Bosco take a serious beating for you. For a man like him, that's not easy. He could have had his men break both of Griffin's arms, but he didn't. If he can show that kind of restraint, he's not a threat to this family. Griffin will see that—once he calms down."

I was grateful Vanessa was on my side because it hadn't always been that way. She had been hesitant about Bosco but gradually changed her mind as time passed. "And my father…your father…"

"If they accepted Griffin, they'll accept Bosco. You'll just have to be patient."

"And I don't know if I could have kids with him. His profession is so dangerous. I don't want my kids around that. I went to the casino with him a couple times, and a psychopath started stalking me."

"Well, I don't think your kids are going to join him at the casino," she said with a laugh.

"When they're adults, they might. I just want a different kind of life, a life that he doesn't want."

"What does that mean?" She brought her water closer to her and took a drink. "What do you want?"

"I want to move out of the city and be a full-time mom. I want to take my kids to school, clean up the house, and see my husband when he gets off work at the office. I want a simple, boring, domesticated life… Bosco isn't interested in that. He likes money, booze, cigars…topless ladies. Stuff like that."

"For one, he quit smoking for you. And two, there's only one topless dancer he cares about."

The corner of my mouth rose in a smile. "It seems like you're rooting for him…"

"I just want my cousin to have the man she wants. I

don't want you to give up on him unless you're absolutely sure."

"I just don't want to regret my decision later," I said. "I don't want to be with him for a few years and then regret it. I don't want to imagine who my husband could have been if I'd just walked away."

Vanessa turned quiet, not having anything else to say.

This was my burden, and I had to deal with it.

"I'll say this," she said. "If this is the man you love, don't worry about our parents. They'll accept him if you wait long enough. Griffin will accept him. I'm not saying it'll be easy, but it'll definitely happen eventually, and all your hard work will pay off. But, if there really is no future with this guy, if you really can't have the family life you want…then you're right. You should end it now and not waste any more time. Because the longer you wait…the harder it's gonna be."

I nodded in agreement, considering everything she said. "You're right."

"Take the rest of the week to think about it. And then…stick with your decision."

BOSCO NEVER MENTIONED THE DAY THAT WAS FAST approaching, and neither did I. As if it wasn't an issue at all, we spent our time making love, eating dinner, and snuggling together on the couch.

I knew he wouldn't mention it because he was confident there wasn't a deadline at all.

He knew I wouldn't leave.

And that would make it all the more painful if I did.

When I was work, I was distracted because I couldn't make up my mind. I knew what I should do, but the right decision and the easy decision weren't always the same. This wasn't a regular relationship that I could enjoy until it ran its course. It was completely different, and the longer I remained, the more chains bound my wrists.

I was at the shop when an unlikely visitor stopped by.

Ronan.

"Hey, what are you doing here?" I asked, giving him a smile as I put down my shears and gloves. "Want to buy some flowers for a special lady?"

He smiled a lot more than his brother. Just in general, he seemed to be the more upbeat one of the two. He wore a dark blue shirt with a black blazer, along with dark jeans. His hands were in his pockets, and he looked handsome with that dark hair and those pretty eyes. "I'm not a flowers kind of guy."

"Chocolates, then?" I teased. "Unfortunately, I don't have those. I would eat them all if I did."

He chuckled. "If I buy some chocolates, they would probably be for me too."

"Then how can I help you? If you're looking for Bosco, he's not here. He's probably at home." I used the term home loosely, referring to my residence as well. It didn't seem like his penthouse anymore, but a place we both shared.

"I'm not here for him. I'm here for you."

"Oh?" Ronan was never a threat to me, so I didn't care about his unexpected visit.

"Have lunch with me, if you don't mind closing up your shop for thirty minutes."

I wasn't sure if having lunch with Ronan would make Bosco jealous, but it would be ridiculous if he were because neither one of us would ever cross the line. Ronan loved his brother, and I wasn't interested in anyone but Bosco. "Yeah, sure. Let's do it."

WE WENT TO A LITTLE CAFÉ WHERE THEY HAD espresso and sandwiches. We both ordered coffee and lunch before we took a seat at a table together. Ronan insisted on paying, and since he wanted to be a gentleman, I allowed it.

The clouds covered the city, and it seemed like rain was in the forecast. The clouds were deep gray and pregnant with rain. I might have to take a taxi back to the shop because I didn't bring an umbrella.

"Are you working today?" I asked, trying to think of something to talk about besides Bosco.

"No. Bosco is working tonight."

I couldn't keep the disappointed look off my face.

"He told me you hate it when he works."

"It's not that I hate when he works," I corrected. "I don't care what he does for a living. I just hate how late he's out. Sometimes he's there until like three in the morning, and I can't sleep when he's gone."

"I assure you, there's nowhere safer in the city than his penthouse. His windows are tinted and bulletproof, plus there're two dozen armed men in the lobby."

"That's not what I'm afraid of."

"Then what are you afraid of?" he asked before he took a bite of his sandwich. Like his brother, he ate with perfect manners and kept his gaze focused on me throughout the conversation.

"I'm not afraid of anything. I'm just used to sleeping with him, I guess. Now it's part of my life, and when it's off, I can't get comfortable. I'm used to the way he keeps the sheets warm. I'm even used to the slight dip on his side from his weight. I know it's stupid, but it's just a habit now."

"I wouldn't say it's stupid. I'd say it's sweet, actually."

I avoided his gaze and drank my espresso, needing the caffeine to pick up my mood despite the gloomy weather. "Are you seeing someone?"

"Not really," he answered. "I go from fling to fling. Nothing ever serious."

He sounded like Bosco before he met me.

"When I meet the right woman, I'm sure things will be different. But I haven't run into her yet."

"Are you looking for her?" I asked.

He shrugged before he took another bite. "Not actively. Anytime I meet someone new, I just assume it's not her. I think if I'm meant to meet her, she'll pop up eventually. They say that's how those things happen… when you least expect them."

I liked that his brother had an open mind about finding the right woman, but he wasn't in a hurry either. If it were meant to happen, it would. No need to rush. "When she's ready, she'll find you."

"And I'll get her chocolates and flowers," he teased.

"Yes. She'll love that."

He finished his sandwich then wiped his fingers with the napkin.

I wanted to ask him what the purpose of this lunch was, but since that seemed rude, I didn't. If Bosco had a problem with this, he would have intervened by now. He knew the moment Ronan stepped inside my shop.

"So…this is the last week, right?" Ronan held his cup with both hands as he looked at me.

I was surprised he brought it up. "Does Bosco talk about it?"

"No, not really."

I wondered if he was lying. He would never throw his brother under the bus, so there was no way to know.

"I hope that this isn't the last week, for my brother's sake." Ronan kept looking at me, like he was trying to gauge my reaction to the whole thing.

I didn't know how to react, so I didn't give any reaction at all.

Ronan kept looking at me.

The silence became tense.

Ronan spoke again. "My brother is head over heels. I'm sure you've figured that out by now."

"And I love him too…" More than Bosco even understood.

"It's the first time I've seen my brother happy since our mom died. He can actually take a joke once in a while. He's actually made an effort to rebuild our relationship. He's…showing all the good qualities I forgot he had."

If Ronan was guilting me on purpose, it was working.

"I don't want to see him get hurt. I don't want him to go back to where he started. Losing you…will probably devastate him even more than losing our mother."

God, he was torturing me.

"So if you're on the fence about it…I want you to know that. I'm at the casino with him a lot. He couldn't care less about the dancers, about the woman who makes passes at him. He never smokes, even when there's no way for you to find out about it. And I don't need to remind you what he did at The Brawl…risking his life just to have the honor of protecting you."

"Ronan, I've never doubted his love…"

"Then I hope I don't have to doubt yours. I know it's complicated with your family. But…give him a chance. He's the best guy I know. Don't leave him. If you don't give up on him, he'll never give up on you."

"Did he ask you to do this?" I asked, skeptical of the possibility.

"No. When he asks me why we had lunch today, I'm gonna tell him I was talking to you about a woman I'm seeing. If he knew I was bothering you about his relationship, which is none of my business, he'd kill me."

I believed that.

"This stays between us. I just want to do whatever I can to make this work."

"Even if it doesn't, you aren't going to lose him, Ronan. He wouldn't slip back into his old ways. He feels really terrible about the way he treated you in the past."

His eyes narrowed in disappointment. "Please don't tell me that's your answer."

"Honestly…I don't know yet."

He bowed his head and sighed. "What is there to know? The man loves you. The man can give you anything you could possibly want—"

"Not anything."

Ronan stared at me for several heartbeats. "Such as?"

"He knows I want a family. And I can't have a family with a man who runs the underworld. It's way too dangerous. I only went to the casino a few times, and I got a stalker out of it."

"Which Bosco took care of."

"Well, if it's my daughter on the line, I'm not gonna

care if it gets taken care of," I snapped. "My dream has been to buy a big house in Tuscany, close to where my parents live, and raise a family. I want to sell my flower shop and be a full-time mom. I want a husband who will come home every night. You think I can live in a house with four kids while my husband is gone until two in the morning?"

Ronan had no rebuttal.

"It's nothing against Bosco. He's a good man with a big heart. I love him very much. Imagining losing him in a few days is enough to make me start crying. That man has become my whole world. But I know I want this more than anything in the entire world…I want my family. I want my four children. Nothing will ever make me change my mind about that."

Ronan bowed his head slightly, speechless. His hands continued to hold the coffee cup before he returned it to the saucer. It was still steaming hot, as was mine. "You need to tell him that, then. Give him a chance to give that to you."

"Ronan, he already knows. I told him what I wanted on our first date. My desires haven't changed. And Bosco will never give up his casino, give up his livelihood, for a domestic life out in the middle of nowhere. That's okay because I understand that's not what he wants. He's never wanted that. We want different things…" As I spoke to Ronan about this, it made me realize what I had to do. It solidified my decision, and I knew nothing could ever change it back. It was a heartbreaking realization, to know that Bosco wouldn't be mine for much longer. "Bosco wants me to be his queen, to continue his life the way it's always been, and come home to me when it's done. But that's not my dream. I don't love Bosco because of his power and his money… I love in him in spite of those things."

Ronan held my gaze, his disappointment heavy.

"I hope you understand, Ronan. I hate this so much…I really do."

He left his mug and plate on the table and turned his head to look out the window. He wasn't angry but bitterly hurt that this conversation ended the way it did. He wanted his brother to be happy, wanted it so much that he actually cornered me in order to have this conversation. "It sounds like you've made your decision, then."

The only reason tears weren't streaming down my cheeks was because we were in public. But the second I returned to my shop, I would lock myself in the bathroom and give myself ten minutes to cry my pain away. "Yes…I'm sorry."

9

BOSCO

EVERYTHING at the casino was still going smoothly. The memory of me mutilating The Butcher was fresh in everyone's minds, so I was still the conversation topic at most poker games. Memberships had increased by thirty percent, and more people wanted a piece of the pie at my casino.

I'd been spending fewer nights there that week, choosing to stay home with Carmen. I knew she wouldn't leave me, but I was acting cautiously anyway. We spent our nights tangled up together in bed, warm under the sheets and sweaty with pleasure. When I looked into those green eyes, I knew I would never want another woman more than her.

She was my everything.

But I couldn't ignore my business altogether, so I'd forced myself to come out tonight. I was standing on the balcony and watching all the men gathered at the tables. The cameras caught the details better than my naked eye, but when I stood over all the members, it added a note of tension all the men could feel—that they were always being watched.

Ronan came to my side, wearing a suit with his hands in his pockets. "Business has increased."

"We've had a hundred new members this week."

Instead of watching the men beneath us, Ronan leaned against the railing and looked at me instead.

"Yes?" I turned to him, unsure what he wanted.

"Two more days?"

I was surprised he was keeping track. "Yes. Two more days until she's mine forever."

Instead of smiling, he narrowed his eyes in disappointment. "You still think she's gonna stay?"

"She loves me." I looked away and stared at the crowd again. "She's happy. She's not going anywhere." We would have a difficult road ahead of us, but it was nothing I couldn't handle. Her father and uncle didn't hate me as much when they left as when they'd arrived. They had to respect me somewhat, considering I treated them so civilly when they stepped onto my property. Griffin nearly broke my skull, but I didn't break his face, so that had to earn some respect too. At the very least, I held no ill will for any member of the Barsetti clan.

Ronan stood beside me with his arms crossed over his chest. He turned quiet and brooding, his mind still on the conversation but also far away at the same time.

With wide shoulders and a powerful chest, he commanded respect in the casino the way I did. He simply took a step back and allowed me to have the spotlight, but he was doing a lot of work behind the scenes.

Maybe I was being too confident about Carmen, but I believed in what we had. I believed in every tear she shed for me, every confession of love she gave me, and everything else beautiful that we shared. I was a man in love, and I wouldn't trade it for anything else in the world. It was the first time I felt complete since my mother died. Carmen filled the gaping hole inside my chest. I used to ignore my feelings and heartache and pretend they didn't exist, but once Carmen arrived, I began to understand just how depressed I was because I was finally happy for the first time in years.

Ronan must have been holding his breath because he let out a sigh that was loud enough to be audible over the sound system. "Bosco, I need to tell you something, and it's not easy for me to say. It'll be even more difficult to hear."

"Alright." I straightened and turned to him, unsure what my brother was struggling to spit out. Was it about the casino or was it about Carmen?

He wouldn't look me in the eye. "When I had lunch with her the other day, we didn't talk about some woman I'm seeing. I made that up."

He lied to me? I gripped the handrail as my eyes narrowed on his face, irritated that my own flesh and blood would betray me like that. When I saw him with Carmen, I thought it was unusual, but I trusted every word that came out of my brother's mouth. Even if his explanation seemed strange, I'd given him the benefit of the doubt. Now I felt like a fool. "Let's hope you have a good reason for that…"

"I actually talked to her about the two of you." He finally turned his head my way so our eyes would lock. "I told her how much you loved her, that you would do anything for her, and I told her this is the first time you've been happy since Mom passed away."

"And why would you say all of that to her?"

"I wanted to make sure she was going to stay. Because you need her, and I need you to be happy."

It was a touching gesture, but I was still pissed.

"So I asked if she was going to stay…" He looked away, like holding my gaze was too painful. "She said no."

As if someone had stabbed a knife right into my stomach, my guts spilled on the floor, and the air left my lungs. I didn't change my expression because we were in public, but I squeezed the railing a little tighter, my knuckles turning white.

"She said she loved you, and she doesn't want to be with anyone else…but it would never work. The two of you want different things."

Love, commitment, and good sex? No, we wanted the same things.

"She said she wants a family, four kids and a husband."

"Who said I wouldn't give that to her?" I'd already offered once. Maybe she didn't take me seriously. I was willing to do anything to keep this woman. She was the key to my happiness.

"I don't think she realizes that," Ronan said. "And if that's the case, you should tell her. But even then, she said she doesn't want to be part of this scene. After what happened with The Butcher, she's afraid for the safety of her kids. She doesn't want you gone all night while she's home alone with the family. She would never ask you to give up all of this because it wouldn't be right…and she thinks it wouldn't be right for you to ask the same of her."

The future had looked so clear earlier that morning, but now it was bleak once more. I was fine before Carmen came along, but I would never be fine again after she was gone. Another woman would never mean anything to me. It would be back to meaningless sex, buying expensive gifts for women because that's what they wanted. I would be absorbed back into the darkness once more. "I can't give up the casino for her." I wanted to pretend her request was ridiculous, but it wasn't. She wanted a quiet and simple life in the country, raising her kids with a man who would always be home by five. She didn't want to be tarnished by my lifestyle, to have a man walk in the door smelling like cigars, booze, and cheap perfume. It all made sense—

but it still hurt like a bitch. "Did she know you were going to tell me all this?"

"I don't know. I never said I was or wasn't."

She was leaving the day after tomorrow, and there was nothing I could do to stop it.

Ronan kept watching me, the concern in his eyes. "I'm sorry, Bosco. I tried to change her mind."

I wasn't angry at him anymore. I had worse problems now. "I know, Ro." I faced the floor again, breaking eye contact because I didn't want to see the pity in his eyes. I gripped the railing with both hands and tried to combat the empty feeling inside my chest. Now I didn't even want to go home, not even if she was naked on my bed. I didn't want to pretend this horrible reality wasn't really happening.

My brother came to my side and faced the same direction. "This probably isn't my place to say, but…this is gonna get old someday."

I stared at the men sitting at the poker tables, holding their cards and tossing their chips into the center. Topless waitresses circulated and waited on the men. Security stood against the walls and kept an eye on everyone. The naked girls danced in the cages as the smoke rose to the ceiling, and the music thudded overhead.

"The women, the booze, the job…all of it will turn stale. When you're in your fifties, this will feel redundant and repetitive. You don't want to stand here in twenty years regretting the choice you made."

"What are you saying, Ronan?"

"Maybe you should give up the casino." He kept hold of the railing the way I did.

"Give up everything and give her what she wants."

The casino was my life; it was my purpose. I loved the power and I loved the money. My identity wouldn't exist without it. "Ro, I'm nothing without it."

"That can't be true. Because Carmen loves you in spite of all this…not because of it. So you must be something to her."

I kept staring at the floor. "What would I do all day? What kind of man would I be? I would just stay home all day and get fat? I love Carmen, but the casino is who I am. I put everything on the line when I started it, and I can't just walk away from that. I refuse to be a man who sacrifices everything for a woman. If she won't sacrifice everything for me, then why should I do it for her?" It didn't matter how much I loved Carmen. Walking away from all of this was not an option. I would be giving up who I was, and one day, I would regret that.

Ronan was quiet, letting my final words fill the air.

Accepting the loss was hard. But losing everything I'd worked so hard for would be even worse.

"Then she's going to leave, Bosco," my brother said. "I just want you to be prepared for it…so you aren't blindsided." He moved his hand to the center of my back, comforting me with the subtle gesture of affection.

I didn't react to the touch.

"I'm sorry." He pulled his hand off my back then walked away.

Now I stood alone on the balcony, my heart starting to throb because the reality hit me like the water from a cold shower. The inevitable was fast approaching, and if just the thought was so painful, how would it really feel in the moment?

How would I let her walk away…for good?

10

CARMEN

IF RONAN TOLD his brother what I said at the coffee shop, it didn't seem like it.

Bosco's behavior hadn't changed. He was the man he was before, but since he was naturally intense and quiet, maybe it was difficult to tell the difference.

I struggled to keep myself together. Tomorrow morning, I would pack up my things and go back to my apartment. I would drive in my little car without twelve men following me. Like this had all been a dream, I would return to my old life and pick up where I left off.

I wouldn't miss the security and the luxury as much as I would miss the man who provided those things. I had amazing sex on a regular basis, but now that would be a thing of the past. It was difficult to imagine going out with some other guy then taking him back to my place. It was impossible to imagine having sex with someone else—and not think about Bosco.

This heartbreak was already killing me, and I hadn't even left yet.

I went into the bedroom and opened the closet, seeing my suitcase open and ready to be filled with my clothes and shoes. I shut the doors again, trying to pretend I didn't see it at all. Once the night passed and morning arrived, this would all be over.

How did time go by so fast?

Bosco's voice sounded from the kitchen. "Beautiful, dinner is ready." Like we were a husband and wife at home after work, he called for me to join him.

I took a deep breath and controlled my emotions, not wanting to cry into the bland meal Bosco prepared.

I went into the dining room and saw a meal I didn't expect. "Wow. Pot roast, potatoes, and…is that actually bread?" I spotted the plate of garlic bread on the table, a fresh loaf sliced up perfectly. My depression was temporarily gone when I looked at the impressive, and edible, meal he made.

He sat down, shirtless in his sweatpants, and smiled. "Yes. It's real bread."

"And it looks so good." I sat down and watched him open a bottle of red wine. He poured two glasses and pushed one toward me. "This should pair well with the meat."

"You're right. Look at you…wine connoisseur."

"I pay someone to figure that stuff out. Personally, I think scotch goes with everything, but that's not romantic, is it?"

I shrugged. "You like what you like, right? It's not like you're smoking a cigar at the table."

He served both of our plates, and then we began to eat. "Not smoking has changed my palate. I can taste things differently now." He placed a piece of bread on his plate. "My scotch has a better kick to it too."

"Good." I hoped that meant he would continue not to smoke after I left. Even if I never saw him again, I wanted him to have a long and healthy life. "Smoking is disgusting. My father used to smoke cigars on occasion, but my mom set him straight."

"Women will do that…"

I took a few bites, and my stomach immediately growled with joy. "This is so good." The chunks of meat were tender, and the carrots and potatoes were cooked to perfection. Wiping my plate with a thick piece of bread just made it better.

Bosco watched me with a slight smile on his face. "They say food is the way to a man's heart. You prove that wrong."

"How so?"

"Well, sex is the way to my heart. And food is the way to yours."

"That's not really accurate. I'm not that obsessed with food. It's just you never have anything good around here, so I get excited when you actually make something decent. You know, that actually has flavor, fat, and carbs."

He gave me an affectionate look. "Men don't look

sexy when they eat fat and carbs. Women can eat whatever they want and still look sexy."

"I disagree, but that's a nice thing to say."

He took another piece of bread.

"It's a big cheat day, huh?"

"The biggest." He drank his wine after a few bites then looked at me as he licked his lips.

I would miss the sex and the affection, but I would miss this most of all—this easygoing relationship. We could have conversations just the way Vanessa and I did. He wasn't just my lover, but my friend. After he dialed down his obsessive behavior and controlling nature, he was wonderful to be around.

As if he knew exactly what I was thinking, he held my gaze and kept eating, a note of sadness to his look. He didn't address what would happen in the morning, maybe because he wasn't sure what would transpire. Perhaps he was still confident I wouldn't leave.

A part of me wanted Ronan to have told him the truth, just so it wouldn't be so unexpected, and therefore, more painful.

Or better yet, I wish I didn't have to leave at all.

It was my bitter heartbreak talking, but I wished I'd never met him. I wished we'd never crossed paths. While I enjoyed our time together, being haunted by the memory would kill me. In this case, it would be better never to have loved at all than loved and lost.

HE KISSED MY BELLY BUTTON, HIS TONGUE SWIRLING around the navel piercing I'd had since my late teens. My mother was disappointed when I got it, annoyed when she first saw me in a bikini. But every man I'd been with loved it, so I didn't have any regrets. Bosco kissed it the best, dragged his tongue up the center of my ribs until he reached the swell of my tits. He kissed both of my boobs, giving each one the attention it deserved. My nipples were sucked hard into his mouth, and he gave me a gentle bite with his teeth.

"Babe…" I was already so wet, so anxious for him.

He moved down my body and pushed my legs back with his large hands. His lips pressed against my most tender place, and he made love to my clit with his mouth, his tongue swirling hard before his kisses turned soft.

No other man had ever done it before him.

I gripped his hips and closed my eyes.

He gripped me back as he kissed me, smelled me. He moved his tongue deep inside me to feel how wet I was, and then he moved farther back and licked my asshole.

I tensed at his touch, surprised by how good it felt. Bosco wasn't afraid to explore me everywhere, to enjoy every inch from head to toe.

He kissed the inside of my thighs and moved up my stomach again, devouring my tits once more until we were face-to-face. He stared down at me, his expression hard because he was filled with arousal, longing, and love. He got into position between my legs, and then he gently slid inside me, his eyes locked on mine.

My hands clutched at his thick arms, and I breathed hard as I felt him push inside me. Inch-by-inch, he moved, stretching me like he was taking my virginity. He pushed until he was all the way inside, a perfect fit in my tightness.

"Bosco." I looked into that handsome face and memorized it, knowing this was what I would think of when I had fun with my vibrator. I wouldn't look at porn. I would remember the best sex I'd ever had, making love to the man who made me weak in the knees. "I love you…" I wanted to say that as many times as I could, to take advantage of the last night I had any right to say it.

"And I love you." He rocked into me slow and gentle, thrusting deep and even. Instead of kissing me, he stared at me with the same love in his eyes. I was the only woman he'd ever looked at like this, ever cherished with just his gaze. I was the only woman he'd ever made love to. "More than anything."

My hand slid up the back of his neck, and I fingered his short hair as I pulled his face to mine and kissed him. "Make love to me all night…" I wanted to ignore the passing moon and the approaching sun. I wanted to pretend there was no tomorrow at all. I just wanted to enjoy this perfect man as much as I could, to hold on to this memory even when I was old and gray and surrounded by my grandchildren.

"I will, Beautiful."

I SLEPT FOR TWO HOURS BEFORE I REALIZED IT WAS morning.

I glanced at the clock on the nightstand and saw that it was ten.

The shop would stay closed today because I would be in no condition to work. And if I did have to work today, I would be so late, there wouldn't be much point going in.

Bosco was already gone from the bedroom.

I got out of bed and felt the weight hit my stomach. The dread was killing me, making my body cramp up and my heart race with fear. So much pain was about to hit me, and my body was preparing for the blow.

I could go out there and have breakfast like it was a normal day, but that would be too painful.

Today wasn't a normal day.

I should just grab my stuff and leave while he was in the other room. It would be cruel to make him watch me pack.

I didn't even want to watch myself pack.

I didn't bother with my hair or makeup, and I tossed all my stuff into the suitcase. I didn't bother taking the designer gowns he'd bought me because I had nowhere to wear them anyway. I left behind the diamonds because it felt wrong to take them. The only reason I had been with him was for him—not the jewels. I refused to taint our relationship with materialistic possessions.

Everything was thrown into the bag haphazardly, not folded neatly like usual.

That didn't seem important right now.

I grabbed my toiletries from the bathroom, throwing away all the things I didn't need so he wouldn't have to look at it. All my makeup and accessories were shoved into a plastic bag and placed on top of the clothes. Once everything was crammed inside, it was nearly impossible to zip the bag shut.

I stood in the bedroom with the suitcase by my side, dreading what would happen next. I didn't want to walk out there, especially when I knew he would be waiting for me. He must have anticipated this based on my behavior last night. It was obvious I was saying goodbye, enjoying him for the last few hours that he was mine.

I steadied my tears because it would hurt more to cry. It would hurt him and myself. The break wouldn't be clean and easy, but it was best to do it as quickly as possible. I ran my fingers through my hair before I grabbed the handle of the bag and moved down the hallway, the rolling suitcase loud against the floor. It announced my presence for me, told him I was bringing all my stuff along for the ride.

Bosco was sitting on the couch, in his usual sweatpants. It didn't smell like breakfast, so he obviously hadn't made anything. With the TV off and the silence surrounding him, he'd been sitting there waiting for me.

He knew.

I stopped in front of the elevator and waited for him to acknowledge me.

He stared at the ground with his head tilted to the floor, refusing to look at me.

I didn't want to say goodbye. I didn't want to say anything at all. It was so painful that neither one of us could deal with it.

Bosco finally rose to his feet and walked toward me. He didn't make eye contact until he was right in front of me, until he was ready to meet my gaze. He gave me a brave stare, doing his best to hide the grief deep in his eyes.

I stared back, my eyes watering.

He didn't say anything. He didn't try to convince me to stay or ask why I was leaving.

The silence passed until a few minutes came and went.

I knew if I opened my mouth, no words would come out. I would just cry instead. So I said nothing, knowing there were no words I could say to make this easier anyway. I wanted to explain that I had to leave, regardless of how much I loved him. But none of that would make a difference in the long run. It would still be painful no matter what I did.

He cupped both of my cheeks and gave me a soft kiss on the mouth. It wasn't packed with fire, lust, and love. It was filled with pain, a gentle kiss that was forced. It was like he didn't want to kiss me at all because it only reminded him that it was the last kiss we would ever share.

When he pulled away, he hit the button to the elevator and typed in the code.

The doors opened.

He didn't look at me as he waited for me to walk inside.

I grabbed my suitcase and stepped through the doors, my heart pounding because I knew this was it.

He grabbed the door to make sure it wouldn't close. "My men are going to take you somewhere first. Your car has already been returned to your apartment." He pulled his hand away, and the doors began to shut immediately. He turned around so he wouldn't have to look at me again, and the last thing I saw was his chiseled back as he walked away.

I descended to the bottom of the building, unsure where his men were taking me and why. Bosco gave me no explanation, and he obviously didn't want to participate in whatever it was.

I really had no clue.

When I stepped into the lobby, his men took my suitcase and purse and placed them in the black car. I was ushered into the back seat before the car was pulled onto the road. When I was in the presence of his men, I kept a stoic expression and hid my emotions deep inside my chest. I didn't want to sob in the back seat, professing my heartbreak to these men who were practically strangers. I didn't even know their names.

The car headed to the west in the opposite direction of my apartment. Then it left the city altogether, heading into the countryside of Tuscany. It was a cloudless day and the sun was bright, but there was still a distinct chill in the air. The storm had made everything beautiful and green.

This was the exact road I took to my parents' house.

The car slowed down as we approached a large gate made of metal. Cobblestone walls surrounded the property, and large trees could be seen on the other side. The actual estate was invisible because it was blocked by all the greenery.

The gates opened, and we drove inside.

Now I really had no idea what was going on.

The car drove down the concrete path until it approached a three-story home that looked like a mansion. Designed in classic Tuscan style, it reminded me of my parents' home. It was surrounded by green plants and gorgeous flowers, all having survived the harsh winter.

The car stopped.

The driver came to the back and opened the door.

I took my cue and got out, inhaling the winter air straight into my lungs. I looked up at the house in the light of the sun, admiring its classic Italian features as well as its European history. There were large double doors at the front.

"Come with me." He walked ahead of me, moving farther up the drive until we were fifty feet away from the car. "Mr. Roth wanted me to give this to you." It was a small box, a rectangular package that could fit across both of my palms.

He walked away and left me alone with the gift Bosco wanted me to have.

I looked at the simple brown box made of leather and admired it, wondering what was inside. Was he giving this house to me? Why would he do that? I'd always told him this was where I wanted to live. Did he actually expect me to accept this gift? To live here with my husband and have my family?

I opened the box and looked inside.

It took me a second to understand what I was looking at.

There was a brown house key, beautiful in its design. It was antique-looking, like it was the original key made for the house. Beside it was something else…a diamond ring. A white gold band with an enormous single diamond in the center, it was simple, sleek…and beautiful. "Oh my god…" I stared at it without touching it, knowing once my fingers wrapped around it, I would place it on my left hand and never take it off.

There was also a note.

I set the box down and unfolded the piece of paper.

It was a handwritten note from Bosco.

Beautiful,

This isn't a proposal.

But this is everything I want to give you, if you'll have me.

The house has five bedrooms. One for us. One for each child you want to have.

This is the diamond ring I want you to wear until you die.

Ronan agreed to take over the casino so I can step back. I'll be home with you every night. I'll be away from that scene for good.

I'll be the kind of husband you want me to be.

Losing the business I built with my bare hands is hard. But losing you is harder.

We have a long way to go. We have a lot of work to do. But I'm in this forever if you are. Come back to the penthouse if you want me. But if you don't…then this is goodbye. Keep the ring so you'll never forget how much I love you.

-Bosco-

My tears stained the paper and made the ink run. "Babe…"

————

When the elevator doors opened, he was already standing there, just feet from where the doors parted. His eyes were wide as if he couldn't believe I was really there until he got a good look at me.

It seemed like he'd been standing there the entire time, waiting for me to turn around.

I'd cried on the drive home. I'd cried in the elevator. And now I was still crying, the brown box held tightly in my hands.

His jaw was tense, and his eyes were hard, the best expression of emotion he could muster. His entire body was tensed like he was ready for a fight, the adrenaline pumping hard in his muscles. He didn't reach out and grab me, afraid I might be an apparition or his imagination.

I stepped out of the elevator with the box clutched tightly in my hand, containing the three things I wanted most in this world—my marriage, family, and his love. That was what I wanted from him, but it was too soon to ask for it. I'd never asked him to leave the casino because it would be wrong if I did.

We'd only been together for four months, and that wasn't long enough to commit for a lifetime.

But with him, it felt like it might be.

He must feel the same way.

"I want all of those things," I whispered through my tears. "You're the only person I want them with. But… are you sure you want to do this? It's a big sacrifice to make, and I wouldn't blame you if—"

"Yes." His hands moved to my arms, and he looked

down into my tear-stained face, his emotions matching mine even if they weren't visible on the surface. "I'm proud of the business I built. I'm proud I could provide for my family. I'm not ashamed of what I do, and I'll never be ashamed of it. But things change…life changes. We can either change with it or get left behind in bitter regret. Losing you…is something I'll regret for the rest of my life."

"Bosco…" I sniffed and wiped away my tears at the same time. "You want kids? I just didn't think…" He didn't seem like someone who wanted to be a father. He only wanted to take care of his business.

"Not right now," he said honestly. "Not next year. But yes…eventually. Whenever you're ready to start, I'll be ready too."

"Because four kids is a lot of kids…"

He smiled slightly with his eyes, not his lips. "Yeah, I think you're a little crazy. But I'll do four…six…whatever you want."

I held the box to my chest, the diamond ring and key inside. "I love the ring…" He wasn't giving it to me yet, but I wanted him to know that I adored it. That I couldn't wait to wear it.

"It reminded me of you the second I saw it."

I looked into his eyes and imagined a future I could see unfolding, a happy one where my husband would always be by my side every single night I went to sleep. But it was still cloudy, because I had no idea how this would work with my family. Now that I'd decided he was the man I was going to marry, it was time to do the hardest part.

Introduce him to my father.

He grabbed the box from my hand and set it on the entryway table. "I know there's only one way you want me to ask you. That's the only reason why I haven't…"

I wanted my father's blessing. I wanted my family to be part of it. I didn't want to do this without them. Being engaged was about combining family members, not keeping them apart. I wanted my father to be happy with the man I chose, to happily give his permission so he'd never have to worry about me again. "I know."

His hands cupped my cheeks, and he pressed his forehead to mine. "You were only gone for a few hours…and I was devastated."

"Me too."

He closed his eyes as he held me. "I never want to go through that again. I know I can give up the casino…because that was so much easier than watching you walk away."

11

BOSCO

CARMEN WAS asleep in my bed—right where she belonged.

It was eleven in the evening, and my phone vibrated on the nightstand with my brother's name on the screen.

I took the call in the living room. "Hey."

"Did she stay?" he blurted out, caring about my personal life in the way Mom would have. Ronan was indifferent about a lot of things, very easygoing and casual. But he was obsessed with Carmen staying as much as I was.

"Yes." My mouth stretched into a grin. "She came back."

"That's great news. I'm happy for you."

I was happy for me too. When I agreed to hand over the business to my brother, it was full of pain and regret. The casino had always been my baby. I worked hard for the respect I earned in that place. Now every-thing was slipping through my fingers. But watching Carmen walk back into my penthouse erased all the bitterness.

None of that stuff mattered anymore.

"She's a great girl," Ronan said. "I really like her. I want her to be a Roth."

"I do too. But we've got a long road ahead of us…"

"Her family?"

"Yeah."

"Have you decided what you're going to do?"

"We haven't talked about it." After we were reunited, we went into my bedroom and never left. As if we hadn't just made love the night before, that's all we did, choosing to communicate with thrusts and kisses.

"When you do talk about it, let me know how that goes."

I was dreading the next step we had to take. Cane and Crow seemed calm when they thought there was a possibility I might go away. But now that I wasn't leav-ing, they might get fired up and do whatever they could to push me out.

I hoped Carmen would fight for me.

"Let me know if you need anything, Bosco."

"Thanks, Ronan."

He hung up.

I sat on the couch in the living room and didn't go back to bed. I hadn't slept much last night, but I suddenly wasn't tired. There was adrenaline in my veins, along with dread and fear. Anytime I wanted something, I usually got it. But in this instance, there was something standing in my way.

Cane Barsetti.

"Are you alright?" Carmen joined me in the living room wearing only my t-shirt. With messy hair and thoroughly kissed lips, she looked like a fantasy.

"Just talking to my brother."

"How is he?"

"Happy we're together."

She sat beside me and pressed her knees together. "Your brother is very sweet. He really loves you."

"I know. I'm very lucky." He had my back even when I didn't deserve it.

"He tried to convince me to stay…tried to make sure I wouldn't leave you."

I nodded. "He told me."

"I thought it was sweet that he would put himself out there like that, confront me and remind me how amazing you are…like there was any chance I would forget."

He was the best guy I knew. I hoped one day I would be able to repay him somehow. "So, where do we start?" The only thing standing in our way was her family, and that was an obstacle that seemed impossible to overcome.

She stared at me for a long time, clearly not having an answer. "I don't know…"

"I intend to keep working at the casino until we

figure it out. When the time comes, I'm prepared to walk away...but I'm not going to do it prematurely." She already had my commitment, so the second everything was ready, I would honor what I'd said. But it didn't seem fair for me to give up everything when we didn't know what would happen with her father. "I hope you understand."

"I do."

"Do you want me to approach your father? I will if you want me to."

"Oh no," she said with a slightly deranged laugh. "No, no, no. That's a terrible idea..."

The only reason I didn't tell her I'd already met her father was because I'd told her father I wouldn't. If I said he marched down here and tried to pay me off, it would hurt their relationship. That was the last thing I wanted, to come between a father and a daughter. But that also forced me to be complicit in a lie. "Then where should we begin?"

"I guess I'll talk to him...just the two of us. I don't want to blindside him by bringing you along. I don't even think I'll get my mother involved in this."

I wondered how Cane would handle it, if he would pretend he'd never met me. He didn't seem like the kind of man who would lie, but he also wouldn't risk upsetting his daughter either.

"I'll talk to him first. See what he says. And hopefully...the two of you can sit down together, and we can go from there."

We'd already sat down together, and he told me he wanted me to disappear. I wasn't good enough for his daughter, despite everything I did for her. Maybe stepping away from this lifestyle would change his mind. Maybe it wouldn't. "Alright."

"Let's talk about it more in the morning." She patted my thigh then left the couch. She sauntered away, her sexy body shifting as she walked in my t-shirt. She headed down the hallway until she rounded the corner.

My phone started to vibrate again. This time, it was a number I didn't recognize.

I answered. "Bosco Roth."

His voice was unmistakable over the line. "Did she stay?" Deep, magnetic, and constantly full of threat, Cane Barsetti sounded just as harsh over the phone as he did when we spoke three weeks ago.

I dreaded the sound of his disappointment. "Yes."

Cane was quiet, dead silent.

"She—"

Click. Cane Barsetti hung up on me, not giving a damn about anything else I had to say.

12

CARMEN

VANESSA WALKED into my shop first thing in the morning. "I called you twice last night."

I hadn't looked at my phone until I left for work today. "I know. I didn't notice it until I got out of the shower this morning."

"Because…?" With both hands on her hips, she walked toward me, her attitude shining in her eyes. "Were you busy last night?"

She wasn't going to rest until she heard the words fly out of my mouth. I set my tools aside and sucked it up to tell the truth. "I was with Bosco last night."

"Oh my god, so you're staying?" She leaned against the counter as she looked at me, her belly a little bigger every single day.

"Yeah."

Vanessa sighed. "What about everything you decided on?"

"Well…" I told her that his drivers took me to the house he'd bought, along with the box that contained his letter and the diamond ring. "He said he was willing to give it all up for me…so I came back."

Speechless, Vanessa stared at me with her mouth gaping open. "Oh my god…"

I couldn't believe it either, even when I was staring at the words on the page.

"He's gonna walk away from everything?"

"Yes…once we're in the clear."

"In the clear?" she asked.

"With my father…your father…the entire Barsetti clan." Each member of my family was just as close to me as all the others. No one felt distant. Conway felt like my brother as much as my own brother did. Our closeness was both a blessing and a curse.

"I see," she said. "Add Griffin to that to-do list too."

"Are you at least on my side?"

She shook her head slightly, like I'd asked a stupid question. "This guy offered to walk away from his world for you. I think he's redeemed himself in my eyes. Plus, he didn't attack my husband even when he had every right to. The guy is a saint. Of course, I'm on your side. But when it comes to our fathers, I'm not sure how much that will help you."

"You know what will help me?" I asked, an idea popping into my head.

"Hmm?"

"Griffin. If Griffin vouches for him…that could completely change everything."

Vanessa shook her head again, but this time, it seemed like she wasn't cooperating. "I have a lot of influence over that man, but I can't make him do something he doesn't want to do. We just had an argument about how I can't be around Bosco without him there. I don't think it's likely his support is gonna happen."

"What if I talk to him?"

She shrugged. "You can try, but I don't think it's gonna help."

"What if we all went to dinner? Maybe that would soften Griffin a bit."

She laughed. "Griffin loves food, but not that much."

"Well, do you have any better ideas?" I had to make this work, and I had to give Bosco the best chance possible. Having Griffin's support could make a huge difference.

Vanessa must have seen the heartbreak in my eyes, because she finally caved. "I'll get Griffin to come to dinner. But that's the best I can do. Have Bosco explain that he's decided to give up everything for you. If that doesn't please Griffin, at least it'll make him respect Bosco."

"Thank you so much. Your father and Griffin are connected at the hip now. If we have Griffin helping us out, Uncle Crow could help persuade my father to get on board with this. It's better than nothing, right?"

"Yeah, you're right. You helped Griffin and me at the start of our relationship. Of course we'll do anything we can to help you."

WHEN I ASKED BOSCO TO DINNER WITH VANESSA AND Griffin, he didn't put up an argument.

He wore a gray V-neck, a black blazer, and dark jeans. His watch was on his wrist, and a spray of his cologne made him smell potently masculine. He was tall, dark, and so handsome it hurt sometimes.

He stood near the elevators and looked at his phone as he waited for me, still running the business as usual. He hadn't gone in to work since I came back to him, and he probably had Ronan handling everything in the meantime.

He looked up at me when he heard the sound of my boots. His eyes roamed over my body in my tight jeans and sweater, affection deep in his gaze. "You look beautiful." His arm hugged my lower back, and he brought me in for a kiss on the corner of my mouth.

He was the one who looked beautiful. "Thanks."

He kissed my forehead before he entered the code on the wall. The doors opened, and we stepped inside. "I wonder if Griffin is gonna punch me this time." He made a joke without smiling, doing his best to lighten the mood even though the comment wasn't funny.

"He won't. I won't let him."

"I would rather you let him hit me than get in the way." His arm wrapped around my waist. "It's a nice way to break the tension. You know, the way men communicate."

I rolled my eyes. "That's barbaric."

"No, Beautiful. You've seen men be barbaric." Without spelling it out, he was referring to the ring when he beat The Butcher into submission. It was like watching wild animals rip each other apart, for sport as well as for glory.

I didn't want to think about that night. "You need to win Griffin over, Bosco."

"Not possible."

"Well, you need to try."

"Griffin isn't the kind of man that changes his mind. That's not a bad thing. He's stubborn and hardheaded because he bases his decisions on instinct. That's what makes him a good killer—because he can read situations so well."

"He's not a killer anymore."

He shrugged. "Still has killer instincts. I know I'll always have them."

We got into the car and were driven to the restaurant. Bosco held my hand in the back seat as he looked out the window, watching the cars pass on the road and the pedestrians on the sidewalk. It was a clear night and the stars were visible, but that also meant it was particularly cold.

We arrived at the restaurant, and Bosco took me by

the hand as he guided me inside. We found Vanessa and Griffin in the corner, sitting at a private table far away from the other diners.

That was best for everyone in the room.

When we reached the table, I hugged Vanessa then hugged Griffin.

Bosco steered clear of Vanessa, not even being polite by shaking her hand. All he gave Griffin was a subtle look and a nod before he pulled out the chair for me.

I sat down, disappointed this was already off to a rough start.

Bosco sat beside me, directly across from Griffin. Unafraid of the beefy man, he held his gaze with a relaxed posture. "Griffin, long time no see."

Griffin didn't seem quite as hostile as before, probably because Bosco didn't go anywhere near his wife. "It hasn't been long enough."

Bosco actually chuckled. "You're a man of few words, but you make every word count."

Vanessa held my gaze then sighed quietly.

Maybe this was a bad idea.

Bosco didn't seem personally offended by Griffin's coldness. He didn't care what anyone thought of him—except for me. "How's Max?"

Griffin's eyes narrowed. "The business has been fine without me."

"Glad they could carry on without you since you were such an integral piece of the team." It wasn't clear what Bosco's angle was, other than to remind everyone, including Griffin, that he used to kill people for a living.

"I only killed people because they paid me to," Griffin said. "You killed people because you wanted to."

"Because they earned the punishment." Bosco handled the conversation with perfect ease. "And I didn't kill them myself. Each opponent had equal odds of success. But I have killed men with my bare hands… but I assure you, they earned it. Maybe my deaths were worse than yours because I didn't get anything out of it besides retribution…or maybe not. I guess we'll never really know."

Vanessa cleared her throat. "Could we not talk about killing people over dinner?"

"There's nothing else to talk about, then," Bosco said. "Because that's all Griffin and I have in common —because we're the same."

Griffin narrowed his piercing blue eyes, clearly provoked by that statement.

So much for Bosco getting Griffin to like him.

"I'm handing the casino over to Ronan," Bosco said without preamble. "We've made our financial decisions, and I'll be stepping away from the business perma-nently—settling down out of the spotlight for good."

Griffin had just as good of a poker face as Bosco, so he seemed indifferent to that statement. "If you're still getting checks, then you're still part of the business."

"He's buying me out," Bosco explained. "The busi-ness will be entirely his."

Griffin still didn't have anything else to say.

"Just as you walked away from your business, I've walked away from mine. We're the same—making sacrifices for the women we love." Bosco had carefully cornered Griffin, so there was no way Griffin could refute anything he said.

"We aren't the same," Griffin said in his baritone voice. "We'll never be the same."

Vanessa spoke up. "You are the same. You may have done different things for a living, but the degree of your crimes is similar. At the end of the day, you both gave up what you loved most for something you ended up loving more. How about we just agree on that?"

Griffin clenched his jaw but didn't argue with his wife in front of us.

"Cut Bosco some slack," Vanessa continued. "The man is doing everything he can to be with Carmen— and not just for a night, but a lifetime. You were persecuted for every little crime you committed by my father and everyone else, but those sins were irrelevant when it came to our love. Bosco just told you he made the ultimate sacrifice to prove his love for Carmen, and you continue to sit there like it's meaningless." She kept staring at her husband. "Let it go, Griffin."

Bosco smiled when Vanessa finished her speech. "I like your wife. She reminds me of Carmen."

Griffin growled so loudly that the rest of the restaurant must have heard.

"I meant that as a compliment," Bosco said. "Didn't mean it in any other way."

"Don't worry about him," Vanessa said. "If any man besides my father says my name, Griffin is offended."

Griffin kept up the same hostile stare, confirming what she'd said.

Bosco turned to me and lowered his voice. "And you thought I was protective…"

I was grateful Vanessa said all that she did because she put everything into perspective for Griffin. "It would mean a lot to me if you would accept Bosco. And it would mean even more to me if you vouched on his behalf to my father."

Griffin wouldn't look at me.

Bosco shook his head. "Beautiful, don't put him on the spot. You can't make a man like another man. That type of affection has to be earned—over a long period of time."

"Tell me why you don't like him," I challenged Griffin. "Give me one good reason that you have nothing in common with him."

Griffin shifted his gaze to me, silent.

I waited for a reason, a justification for his behavior.

Griffin couldn't give a single example. "Just because he and I are similar doesn't mean I have to approve of him. Carmen, I want the best man for you. You're beautiful, smart—"

Now it was Bosco's turn to growl.

Vanessa chuckled. "Two can play that game, Griffin…"

Griffin kept talking. "You deserve the best. You're a Barsetti woman. And Barsetti women deserve—"

"Strong, fearless, and loyal men," Bosco finished. "I'm all of those things. I killed a man in her honor. I protect her every single minute of every day. I provide the kind of life a queen would envy. Not only that, but I've made sacrifices to earn her, bent over backward just so I could have the honor of loving her. There's nothing more I can do to prove myself to you. The least you could do is admit that I'm not a threat to her or any of you. You don't have to like me, and I don't care if you never do. But you have to be honest about my qualities and give me the respect that I'm due." We hadn't even ordered our drinks yet, and Bosco was making speeches that turned everyone silent. "You're the kind of man that doesn't lie, so go to Crow and Cane, and when they ask what you think of me, you have to say I'm not a threat to Carmen or anyone else. You have to tell them I love her—because you see it written all over my face."

THE END OF THE DINNER WAS JUST AS INTENSE AS THE beginning. The men split the bill, and then we walked outside into the frigid air. It didn't seem like the hostility between the two of them had subsided.

But at least Griffin didn't object to him anymore.

"I'll see you later," Vanessa said. "Let me know when you talk to your father. You know I'm going to want to be prepared for the questions my father will bombard me with."

"Yeah, I will." I hugged her back before I moved to Griffin next.

To my surprise, Vanessa moved to Bosco then hugged him. "Even if everyone never likes you, just know that I like you."

Bosco hugged her back awkwardly, clearly tense that Griffin was staring right at them.

Griffin hardly hugged me because he was too focused on what he was looking at.

Vanessa pulled away then rolled her eyes at her husband. "Get over it, Griffin. He's a nice guy. Now let's go home because I need to take my vitamins."

Griffin watched her walk away for a moment before he caught up with her, not saying another word to either of us.

Like magic, Bosco's men pulled up to the curb, and we got inside the car.

I was happy to be inside the warm vehicle with the heated leather seats because the winter air was chilling. The summer could be hot and unforgiving, but I missed it so much now. The only nice thing about the winter months was having a man to keep me warm.

We headed back to the penthouse in silence.

"I think that went well," Bosco said in a teasing manner.

"I think you made as much progress as you're going to make."

"He knows I'm right. He might not like me, but he doesn't have a justification to reject me. He won't be a problem for us."

"You don't think so?" I asked, a note of hope in my voice.

He shook his head. "No. I treat you well. I take care of you. I clearly love you. Regardless of his personal disagreements, he really has no case anymore. I wouldn't worry about him. He won't oppose me. He may not vouch for me...but silence is better than his objection."

"Then I guess I'll talk to my father next."

"When?" He turned his head toward me, watching my expression.

It didn't matter where or when the conversation took place, my father wouldn't be happy about Bosco. It would take him a while to calm down, but I had to start somewhere. The sooner I started, the sooner it would end. "Tomorrow. I'll go by his office."

13

GRIFFIN

CROW AND CANE were already drinking even though it was only noon. A decanter was on the table along with three glasses. Theirs were already full, and when Crow saw me walk in, he filled my glass without looking at me.

I took a seat, seeing the way Cane was visibly miserable over Carmen. He placed the cool glass against his temple even though there was no ice in it. He must have a migraine, but it was obviously from stress, not dehydration.

Crow watched his brother, leaning back on the leather sofa. "I'm sorry, Cane."

After I'd married Vanessa, I became the third member of their group. They included me in everything, whether it was business or personal. I was the third Barsetti even though I had a different last name. Maybe Conway and Carter would be included if they took over the winery, but since it was me, I was the one who was there all the time. Gradually, I developed a special bond with each of the men, even seeing Cane as somewhat of a father figure. Not nearly as much as I did with Crow, but it was still there.

I had started to see that Cane was similar to his brother, and even though he had more emotional outbursts and rushed decisions, it was only because he cared more. When it came time to protect his family, Cane was the quickest one to jump into the fray. He was impulsive because he was so invested. Caring too much was actually his weakness.

Crow as just more pragmatic about his behavior.

Cane set the glass down. "She could have any man she wants. Literally. And she picks him? Motherfuck-er…" He added more scotch to his glass even though he hadn't finished what he was sipping. "It's only a matter of time before she confronts me about it. What the hell am I supposed to say? Just be fine with it?" He took a long drink, washing down all his liquor in one go. "How does this even happen? She's in a city with hundreds of thousands of people, and he's the one guy she actually likes? Why are arranged marriages outdated? They make perfect sense, if you ask me."

Crow grinned slightly but restrained himself from laughing. "I get why you're angry, but I really think you just have to be okay with it. When she talks to you…let it be."

"Let it be?" Cane asked incredulously. "I'm just

supposed to be thrilled she decided to be with a crime lord?"

"We aren't any better," Crow said simply. "Remember the kind of men we used to be? You tried to kill my wife. I actually hit my own wife. Come on, we were fucking assholes. For some reason, our wives loved us anyway. Look where we are now. Pussy-whipped, romantic, and protective fathers who only care about our families."

"I'll be the first one to admit my wife deserves better," Cane said. "Pearl deserves better. But my daughter definitely deserves better. She deserves fucking Prince Charming. Is there such thing? Was that just some myth?"

"All men are the same." I spoke up. "We're all pigs. We're all dogs. And we're all selfish assholes who only care about a handful of things. The difference between a man and a good man is simply a woman. When a man meets the right woman, he's inspired to be better. He's inspired to be kind, loving, and devoted. Until that moment comes, there's no motivation. Bosco is no different. He was an asshole in the beginning. But Carmen is clearly the right woman for him…because he rose to the occasion." I drank from my glass then let it rest in my hand. "I understand you want Carmen to have someone better. I wanted the same thing. But the truth is…I don't know if that's possible. I know I love and deserve Vanessa, but that only happened because I worked for it. I was different before I met her. But I swear—" I snapped my fingers. "The moment I met her, I changed. And I was never the same again."

Both men watched me, hanging on to my every word.

Cane spoke next. "My daughter will never be safe with a man like that. Any man in this country would want his head on a platter so they can take all his glory. My daughter can't have the life she deserves if she's always looking over her shoulder."

"He gave it up." I set my glass down. "He told me his brother bought him out. The casino is his brother's now. It's not official yet, only if this works out for him. But I can tell he means it. This isn't some kind of act."

Crow was speechless, rubbing his fingers against his temple. He turned to his brother next.

Cane seemed disappointed, not relieved. "Shit."

"You're stuck," Crow said. "Fighting it will just make it worse. Trust me on that."

"This guy isn't like Griffin," Cane argued. "He's pompous and arrogant. He thinks he's the king of this city."

"Because he is." I would never say it to his face. "The man owns everything and everyone. It's a double-edged sword. He has the resources to protect Carmen, but he also brings the risk of attracting danger at the same time."

"If he's willing to give up that lifestyle…" Crow shrugged. "Then he must be pretty serious about Carmen. He's trading in a life of power for a simple one with Carmen. It's the same sacrifice Griffin made, but Bosco's doing it much quicker."

"Because he knew that was the only way to keep Carmen," I said. "She left him at first, but he vowed to give her everything she wanted if she stayed."

"And what else does she want?" Cane asked.

"A husband, four kids, and a house in Tuscany near you," I answered, knowing that would touch him.

Cane didn't show any emotion. "I've been dreading this day for a long time. I told myself it wouldn't be that bad, that I was just making a bigger deal than necessary. Nope, it's worse."

"It doesn't have to be worse," Crow said. "Just be calm. Listen to her. And work toward accepting him. Don't throw a fit like I did."

"I don't know if I can do that, Crow." Cane shook his head. "I just want her to have a good life…"

"She stopped being a child when she was eighteen," Crow reminded him. "She's twenty-five now. She's a smart girl who runs her own business, and in Bosco's defense, he doesn't seem that bad. It seems like he really does love her."

Cane shook his head. "Who knows…"

"He let us go," Crow reminded him. "He never threatened us. He never pointed a gun at us. He didn't take the money. He's walking away from the casino…I know you don't want to accept it, but you have to, Cane. When Carmen talks to you, put on a brave face. Don't push her away. It's not gonna change anything besides putting a strain on your relationship with your daughter."

"My relationship with my little girl is stronger than that," Cane said, offended.

Crow gave him a sad look. "I know this is hard to hear, Cane. But she's not your little girl anymore."

Cane filled his glass then took a long drink, ignoring his brother's words because he didn't know what else to do. He swallowed the liquor hard then slammed his glass back on the table. "She'll always be my little girl."

14
___

CARMEN

BOSCO WALKED me to the elevator.

I hit the code on the wall so the doors would open, but I didn't step inside. I turned around and faced the handsome man with the pretty blue eyes. Everything about him was rough, from his body to his personality. But those eyes shone like two orbs that would fit right on a Christmas tree.

His hands in his pockets, he stood in only his sweatpants. He was shirtless with a hard chest and flat stomach, and his tanned skin looked kissable anytime he was half naked. He gave me a sympathetic look, like he knew I was about to do something extremely difficult. "You're sure you want to do this?"

"It's the next step." I had to start somewhere, and speaking to my father one-on-one was the best way to do that.

"Are you sure visiting him at the winery is the right approach?"

"If I do it at home, my mom will be there."

"Isn't your mother the most reasonable one of the two?"

"Generally, yes," she said. "But my father handles things better when he's alone. I suspect my mother won't be difficult about this, so I don't need to worry about her." I'd always imagined this day quite differently. I would casually tell my parents I was seeing someone, and they would invite him over for dinner. That would be the end of it. But now I needed to tell my father exactly who Bosco was and make him understand this was what I truly wanted.

Bosco continued to stand there, handsome and focused. "I wish I could help you with this."

"I think you would just make it worse, honestly."

He raised an eyebrow.

"Not like that," I blurted. "I just mean, if my father recognizes you, he'll be uncomfortable the entire time."

He gave that cute lopsided grin. "He would recognize me."

"Then all the more reason for you not to come…it might give him a heart attack."

"Your father is tougher than that, Carmen."

"Not when it comes to me…"

He leaned in and kissed me on the cheek. "I'll see you when you get back."

"Alright." I squeezed his arm before I stepped into

the elevator. I made it to the lobby then hopped into my car and made the drive out to Tuscany. It was another beautiful but cold day. My windows were slightly clouded from the frost. I drove through the green fields and the beautiful vineyards until I arrived at the family winery.

I ran into Griffin first. "Hey."

Instead of greeting me the way he used to, he seemed disappointed I was there. "Your father is in his office in the other building." He knew exactly why I was there. It was unlike me to stop at the winery randomly, especially when I had a business to run.

"Thanks…"

Griffin walked off, heading to the main building where my uncle was.

I took the cobblestone pathway and stepped inside the other building. It was a newer addition to the property, built about ten years ago. I walked to his office in the corner and tapped my knuckles on the door.

"Yeah?" my father asked, clearly annoyed.

I opened the door and stuck my head inside. "You got a minute?"

Instead of smiling and showing his excitement to see me, he seemed horrified. He looked at me like he couldn't believe I was standing in his office, even though I'd been there dozens of times before. He must have been having a bad day because it was not the kind of greeting I was used to. "Uh…"

I stepped farther inside, surprised by my father's reaction. "Everything alright?"

Flustered, he ran his hand through his hair and sighed under his breath. "I've just got a lot of things to do today. Meetings, distribution…I was just about to walk out the door."

"Oh, when will you be back?"

"I'll be gone all day," he blurted. He stood up abruptly and grabbed his stuff off his desk. "Shouldn't you be at work?"

I couldn't help but be offended by my father's behavior. Normally, he dropped everything when I walked in. I was his whole world, and he made that known every single time we were together. But now I felt like a nuisance to him. "I just wanted to talk to you about something…"

"Sorry, Carmen. Today isn't the best."

"Should I come back tomorrow, then?"

"Uh…I'm not sure. We'll play it by ear."

"Alright…" I walked out of his office and headed down the path, unsure what to think about that odd conversation. My father was always calm and self-assured, not flustered and clearly annoyed. It didn't seem like I was even his daughter, just another worker who would get him sidetracked. I tried not to let it get to me since my father had always been so loving my whole life. Maybe this was just an off day.

I crossed paths with Uncle Crow next.

"Hey, sweetheart." My uncle greeted me with more

love than my own father did. He gave me a smile then a hug. "What are you doing here?"

"I came to talk to my father, but I guess he's busy today."

His smile immediately fell. "Oh…"

"It seems like he's stressed about something, so I'll try tomorrow or another day."

Crow sighed then gave me a gentle pat on the back. "Yeah…maybe a different day."

BOSCO WAS STANDING IN THE LIVING ROOM WHEN THE elevator doors opened. "That was fast—too fast."

"I didn't talk to him." I walked inside then kissed him on the mouth, greeting him like a woman greeted her husband. "He said he was too busy today, which is strange for him because it doesn't seem like he's ever busy. He always says having Griffin around has made him and my uncle bored, so…I don't know."

Bosco's expression hardened, a clear look of sadness on his face. It was obvious in the way his eyes narrowed slightly, in the way his shoulder slumped as he wrapped his arm around my waist. "I'm sorry, Beautiful."

"It's okay. I didn't want to talk to him about this if he's in a bad mood anyway. I'll wait for a better time."

"Yeah…good idea."

A FEW DAYS LATER, I STOPPED BY THE WINERY AGAIN.

I came to my father's office and knocked, but once again, I was met with a version of him I hardly recognized.

"I'm sorry, Carmen. I'm heading to a business meeting right now, and I won't be back until the end of the day." Like he was about to walk out the door, he grabbed his jacket and his coat. Just like the other day, I wasn't greeted with a hug or even a smile.

It was as if he couldn't wait to get away from me.

"Oh…" I didn't hide my disappointment this time, annoyed that it was this hard to get fifteen minutes of my father's time. "Maybe I can come by for dinner—"

"Your mother and I are pretty busy. We're doing some stuff with Luca." He had an excuse for everything, blocking me at every opportunity.

It seemed disrespectful to accuse him of doing this on purpose, so I held back my assumption, knowing my father would never avoid me on purpose. It used to seem like he couldn't spend enough time with me. He gave me a diamond necklace just a couple months ago. What could have changed in that time? "Well, could you let me know when there's a good time? You must have some time this week…"

He wouldn't look me in the eye, treating me like a gnat that wouldn't go away. "I'll let you know, Carmen. I really should get going." He walked out of his office like he couldn't get away from me quick enough.

As if someone had punched me in the stomach, I

felt winded and sick. I considered myself lucky because I always knew how much my parents loved me. My classmates weren't always so fortunate. My parents loved me no matter what, regardless of the decisions I made in life. That was something invaluable, something I couldn't put a price on. But now it'd been taken away from me—overnight.

I had no idea what I'd done wrong.

WHEN I STEPPED OFF THE ELEVATOR, I TOSSED MY purse onto the couch and yanked off my boots.

Bosco rose from the couch and watched me, concern in his eyes. "Couldn't talk to him today either?"

"Nope." I threw my boot on the ground because I was so annoyed. "He said he had to go to a meeting. When I suggested we have dinner, he said he was too busy for that too. Then I told him to pick a time that was good for him…and he pretty much blew me off. What the hell?" I kicked off my other shoe then placed my hands on my hips. "I love my father and think he's a great man, but…why is he being such an asshole? It's not in his character at all. I just don't understand. I keep thinking I did something to piss him off, but if I did, he would just tell me. He's always been honest and straight to the point." I marched toward the bedroom, not caring about the mess I'd just made in his million-dollar penthouse. Clothes dropped on the way, and by the time I made it to the bed, I was in my underwear. It wasn't even five yet, but I was ready for bed. I was ready for this day to end. I was questioning my relationship with my father entirely, something I'd never done before.

Not once.

Bosco joined me a minute later, getting into bed next to me and spooning me from behind. He wrapped his arm around my waist and pressed his face into the back of my neck. He didn't try to comfort me with words. He didn't try to take off the rest of my clothes either. He just lay with me.

Making me feel less alone.

15

BOSCO

I MET Ronan at the casino.

"Why do you look like hell?" he asked bluntly. "Just a few days ago, you were happy."

"Cane is pissing me off." I walked past him and stepped into the elevator.

He joined me. As we descended to the underground office, he spoke. "What'd he do?"

"More like what he didn't do. He's a fucking pussy. Carmen keeps trying to talk to him about me, but he refuses to have the conversation. He doesn't want to deal with it, so he keeps avoiding her, like he can stop his worst nightmare from coming true." I'd expected things to progress slowly with her family, but I didn't think I would be met with a man who refused to acknowledge my relationship with his daughter.

The elevator stopped at the bottom, and we took the stairs to the office.

He chuckled. "That's one way to handle it. Pretty clever, honestly."

"It's hurting Carmen, so I don't think it's clever." I sat in the leather chair behind my desk. "I didn't think he could stretch it out very long, but somehow, he's managed."

"What are you going to do?" He sat on the black sofa and helped himself to my booze. "Just wait it out?"

I hated seeing the way it affected Carmen. It made me rethink her entire relationship with her father. She wanted to come clean about her love for me, but Cane refused to listen to it because I wasn't good enough for her. The only person it was hurting was his daughter. "No. I'm gonna give him a piece of my mind." I grabbed my phone and made the call.

Ronan's eyes widened in surprise. "Oh…this should be good."

I listened to it ring three times before he finally answered. It was late in the evening, so he probably had to maneuver away from his wife to get some privacy. When he picked up, his tone was loaded with distaste.

"Asshole, do you know what time it is?" he hissed.

"I'm not the asshole who rejects my daughter every time she tries to talk to me."

That silenced him.

"I don't care that you don't like me, Cane. But I care about Carmen. This behavior is ripping her apart. She's confused and doesn't understand why you're shutting her out. I know you don't want to acknowledge me, but you need to acknowledge her. Knock it off." I hung up and set my phone on the desk.

Ronan couldn't suppress his laugh. "That was some interesting ass-kissing…"

"I'm not gonna kiss his ass. Carmen is the most important thing in my life, and I'll stand up for her when she needs me to—even if my opponent is her father. He knows his behavior is inexcusable, and I'm not putting up with it. I'm devoted to his daughter, not to him."

Ronan filled another glass then stood up to hand it to me. "Hopefully, he sees it that way…but I doubt he will."

16

CARMEN

I'D GIVEN up trying to talk to my father.

Hopefully, his mood would pass, and he would behave normally again. Whatever his problem was wasn't my problem. If he found out about Bosco in the meantime and got angry about it, I wouldn't feel guilty.

Because I'd tried to come clean.

I was at the shop when my phone started to ring.

And my father's name was on the screen.

Finally. This better be some good news. "Hey, Father." I stood behind the counter and watched the pedestrians pass on the sidewalk. People were taking advantage of the sunshine as long as they possibly could before the rain inevitably returned.

"Hey, sweetheart." His tone was gentle, like a drop of rain on a rose petal. He wasn't flustered or annoyed like he'd been all week. He sounded like himself but with a hint of disappointment. "I'm sorry about earlier this week…things were just crazy."

"I hope everything is alright." I'd never seen him act that way in my whole life. I always felt like the priority. Not work.

"Yeah…it's better now. So, you want to come by and have that conversation?"

Now that the moment had arrived, I dreaded it all over again. His complete attention would be on me, and I would have to deal with his wrath. There was no doubt in my mind he wouldn't like Bosco. "Yeah, sure."

"Okay. Because I have a few things I'd like to say to you too."

———

BOSCO CALLED ME DURING THE DRIVE. THE SOUND came through my speakers due to the Bluetooth. "Where are you going?"

His men tailed me twenty-four hours a day. There was nowhere I went without them knowing about it. "My father called…and invited me to the winery so we could finally have that talk." I sighed as I drove with both hands on the wheel, my sunglasses on the bridge of my nose. "So, this is really happening…wish me luck."

"Good luck, Beautiful. I'll be waiting for you when you come home."

Good. It would be nice to have a shoulder to cry on.

"Love you," he said, something he rarely said on the phone.

"Love you too."

He hung up first.

I drove the rest of the way, enjoying the beautiful scenery without really taking it in. I was too focused on my destination, too focused on the mission I had to complete. There was no doubt in my mind it wouldn't go well. But how badly it would go…that was still up in the air.

I arrived at the winery twenty minutes later and walked to the building where my father's office was. Griffin and Crow weren't walking around, so they were probably taking care of business elsewhere.

I made it to his office, and this time, the door was open.

My father was sitting behind his desk and looking out the window. There was nothing in front of him, no pens or papers. It was completely clear with the exception of the picture frame holding a photo of the four of us. One elbow was on the desk while his fingers were propped against his check. He was as still as the air outside the window, staring at nothing and looking so tranquil. He was clearly waiting for me, clearing his schedule because he finally recognized I needed to talk to him.

"Hey." I stepped inside with one hand on the strap of my purse, needing something to hold on to. My palms were sweaty in distress as I dreaded the conversation we were about to have.

My father seemed to know this wouldn't be a pleasant talk since he didn't rise from his desk to greet me with a hug. He turned in his chair so he could face me, lowering his hand from his cheek and clearing his throat. "Hey, sweetheart. Please shut the door."

I did as he asked, hearing the door click into place before I sat in one of the armchairs facing his desk.

He slumped in his chair as he looked at me, his face heavy with decades of stress that hadn't been there a few weeks ago. Now he seemed exhausted, like he'd been working so much he'd tired himself out. He sighed as he looked at me, his green eyes showing a million emotions at once. "I think I should talk first."

Why was that? "Is everything alright?" It seemed like we were thinking two different things, having two separate conversations at the same time. There was no way he knew why I was there. The second he knew I was sleeping with Bosco, he would have confronted me about it.

My father sidestepped the question. "I've been avoiding you because I didn't want to have this conversation. I'm not an idiot. I knew I couldn't postpone it long enough to make it disappear entirely. I just…was a coward."

I was even more confused now. "What conversation do you think I want to have?"

He rubbed his fingers across his jaw, feeling the

coarse hair from his shadow of a beard. "There's something I need to tell you, Carmen. I'm not proud of what I did. And I hope you keep in mind that I'm just a father who wants the best for his daughter. Maybe that's not clear all the time…but those are my intentions."

"Okay…now you're scaring me." What did my father do?

He dropped his fingers and held my gaze. "I know about Bosco Roth."

My heart immediately fell into my stomach, sinking like a heavy weight. This entire time, I'd thought my secret was safe, but my father had figured it out. How long had he known? Was he avoiding me for that reason? I didn't try to make up excuses for not telling him as long as I did. My father had been keeping a secret from me just as I was keeping one from him. "How long?"

"A little over a month."

My eyes widened automatically, and a thunderstorm of stupidity struck me. An entire month had passed, and my father had known about the man I was seeing. He knew before I even decided to stay with Bosco. "How did you find out?"

"I wasn't spying on you," my father said. "One of my new clients is the owner of Giovanni's. He told me you and Bosco went there for dinner…and you were sporting that black eye."

I remembered when Bosco ordered a bottle of Barsetti wine for the table. I hadn't even made the connection at the time. I was more engrossed in the man across from me than the situation. Now it all made perfect sense.

"I assumed he was the reason for your black eye…so naturally…I declared war against him."

Obviously, nothing had happened because both men were still living. My father must have calmed down at some point. "He wasn't. Bosco would never lay a hand on me." He was my protector and my provider, not my abuser. "In case that wasn't clear."

"It wasn't clear until Griffin explained the situation to me."

That was a bomb I wasn't prepared for. "Griffin told you?" So this entire time, my father knew, and Griffin didn't care to mention that to me?

"Before you get angry at Griffin, understand he did it for a reason." My father spoke so calmly that it was actually frightening, like he was considering his words very carefully so he would remain in control. "I grabbed my weapons and met up with Crow. I was prepared to march down there and shoot Bosco in the head. Griffin told me everything so I wouldn't go through with it. He explained to me that Bosco didn't give you the black eye, that you two actually had a relationship."

I was still pissed at Griffin for leaving me in the dark, but now I didn't feel completely betrayed. I wouldn't have wanted my father to get himself killed or shoot the man I loved. It was probably the only option Griffin had at the time.

"I'm not gonna lie, sweetheart. I wasn't happy when Griffin told me you were seeing Bosco." He held my gaze, the pain burning in his eyes. "I understand you're an adult who can make your own decisions, but…you couldn't have picked a worse man to get involved with."

His disappointment hurt me, much more than I expected.

"There's something else I need to tell you, and you aren't going to like it. But I don't want to lie about it, regardless of how bad it makes me look."

What did he do?

"Crow and I went to the casino so I could confront Bosco myself."

Now I wasn't breathing, taking in all this information without being able to truly understand it. My father and uncle were in the casino with Bosco…and Bosco never told me. I didn't know whom I felt more betrayed by…Bosco or my own family.

"We spoke for about thirty minutes." My father kept talking calmly, like it was all he could do to combat his true anger. "I told him I didn't like him. I told him I wanted him to leave you alone. And I offered him a hundred million if he cooperated."

I was punched in the stomach—again.

"He didn't take it."

"Of course he didn't," I said, my voice rising. "There's nothing you could offer him to make him leave me. He loves me, Father."

Pain moved into his eyes. "And I love you too, Carmen. I did it to protect you."

"To protect me?" I asked incredulously. "So if he took the money and dumped me, you would have just never said anything?"

"If he took the money, then he never loved you anyway."

I threw my hands down on my thighs. "That's not the point! I can't believe you interfered like that. You didn't even know him. I'm twenty-five years old. How could you treat me and my personal life like you own me?" I'd never been more disappointed in my father, not ever.

He dropped his gaze, unable to look at me anymore. "I knew you would be angry…and I'm sorry."

"You're sorry?" I asked incredulously. "You're sorry that you completely overstepped your bound-aries and stuck your damn nose where it didn't belong?"

"Don't curse at me——"

"Don't threaten my man." I slammed my hand on his desk. "Who the hell do you think you are?"

"Your. Father." He leaned forward, losing his calm-ness. Now his nostrils flared in rage, like a wild bull about to charge. "I admit I shouldn't haven't handled it that way, but I didn't understand the extent of your relationship at the time."

"Then why didn't you ask me? Your daughter?"

"Because Griffin told me to keep it a secret. I

thought I could fix this without you even knowing about it."

"Fix it?" I asked incredulously. "There's nothing to fix. I would have been devastated if I'd lost him."

My father grimaced, like he didn't like that reaction. "Carmen, look. I'm sorry. I'm apologizing to you for what I did. I was upset and emotional at the time, unable to think straight. You're everything to me, and I just…snapped."

I should pity him, but I didn't. Now I was also pissed at Bosco because he knew about all this but didn't tell me. "What happened when you were there? You know, after you tried to buy him off?"

My father ignored my sarcasm. "We talked."

"About…?"

"He told me that you meant a lot to him, that he protects you and respects you."

"Which he does," I said proudly.

"But he also told me how you guys met, how you tried to leave him, but he wouldn't let you, that he forced you to give him a chance."

I admired Bosco for being so honest about it.

"Do you understand how much that pissed me off? Hearing some pompous little bitch say he forced my daughter to do something?"

"It wasn't like that… I wanted to stay." I couldn't tell my father the extent of my feelings, not without making it extremely awkward. "I knew it wouldn't work out with us in the long run…so that was why I wanted to leave. I didn't want to get invested in a guy when there was no future. But I wanted to be with him a little while longer…and that contract was how I got what I wanted."

He pinched the bridge of his nose with his thumb and forefinger. "That's not how relationships are supposed to be. That's not how a woman should talk about her future husband. You want a good man, not a bad man like that."

"He's not a bad man, Father. He's kind, generous, and loving. He's strong, powerful, and extremely authoritative. Maybe you don't want to hear it, but he reminds me of you and Crow. He's a man's man… I don't want an average good guy. I've dated lots of other men, and not a single one made me actually feel something. I understand you had in mind what kind of man you wanted me to be with…but that's not what I want."

"Carmen." He rubbed his temples with his fingers. "This guy is the most famous criminal in Italy. Maybe even in Europe. He's the leader of the crime lords. He has more power and more money than anyone else… combined. Do you really think it's a good idea to get involved with someone like that?"

"I know that's how he is on paper…but he's not like that in reality."

"Yes, he is," he said coldly. "It's one thing to be with a man like Griffin. His occupation is separate from his personal life. But Bosco is the job. He's the symbol of power and authority. That's dangerous."

"He said he would give it up for me."

My father didn't seem surprised by that revelation, only annoyed. He rubbed his temple again before he looked back at me. "I heard."

"Then you're getting what you want."

"I still don't think he's good enough for you, Carmen. Just because he's walking away doesn't mean people don't still want to kill him."

"I'm sure he'll keep his security detail. He's a very paranoid man."

"And he should be," he snapped. "That man has a lot of enemies."

"He's a man of his word, so I doubt it."

"Any man with money has enemies, Carmen."

"What about you and Uncle Crow?" I demanded. "We've had nothing but trouble for the past year."

"I know," he said with a growl. "And I don't want it to continue."

I didn't know what else to say to him. It seemed we'd reached a stalemate. My father wasn't happy about this, and he'd had plenty of time to think about it.

He crossed his arms over his chest as he stared at me. "This is really hard for me, sweetheart. If I didn't give a damn, I would just accept it and look the other way. But you're my only daughter…and I love you more than I can express in words." His eyes softened, full of eternal love and affection. "I know we can't always choose who we fall in love with. Sometimes it's a chemical reaction we can't control. But I want you…to have the best man on this goddamn planet. I want a son-in-law who will protect you when I can't do it anymore. I know you're angry with me, but please remember, my heart is in the right place. It's always been in the right place."

I was emotional and angry at the same time, and his speech softened me just a little bit. "I tried not to fall in love with him. I really did. I knew you would never like him...that Uncle Crow would never like him. I knew this would be a repeat of Griffin and Vanessa. But it happened anyway. I don't want you to hate him. I told him if my family can't look past this...then we don't have a choice."

My father regarded me with a tender expression. "You would choose me over him?"

My eyes watered the second he asked the question. "In a heartbeat. But it would hurt me so much to do it...because I love him. It's real love. It's not lust or infatuation. I know him, know his soul. Don't make me lose him. Don't put me through what Vanessa went through." I wiped my tears away and sniffed back the drips threatening to escape from my nose.

He rose out of his chair then sat in the chair beside me, moving close. Now the conversation felt more natural, not like he was the executioner and I was going to get my head chopped off. He grabbed my hand and held it on my knee. "I don't want to go through what my brother went through with Vanessa. I don't want you to go through what Vanessa went through either.

But…I'm still struggling with this. When I met Bosco, he wasn't as bad as I thought he was going to be, but I still don't like the guy."

"Get to know him."

He sighed like he didn't want to.

"Please," I said. "At least try. If you try and don't change your mind…I'll understand. But you need to give him a chance. Griffin was hated by everyone, but then he turned out to be the greatest addition to this family. Bosco could be the same."

"Griffin is an honorable man. I don't think it's right to compare Bosco to him…just yet."

"Then let's take baby steps. Can you do that for me?"

Father stared at my hand as he considered it, noticeably quiet and tense.

I waited patiently.

After what felt like an eternity, he finally agreed. "Okay…I'll try."

WHEN I CAME HOME, MY EYES WERE PUFFY AND RED. I tried to fix my makeup in the rearview mirror of the car so Bosco's men wouldn't see my tear-stained face, but there wasn't much I could do without my concealer.

I took the elevator up to the top, and the second the doors opened, he was standing there. With his head several inches higher than mine and a concerned look on his face, it was obvious he'd been thinking about me the entire time I was gone. His eyes narrowed slightly when he took in my pained expression. "Beautiful."

"I'm pissed at you right now." I lacked any conviction whatsoever as I walked around him and stepped into the apartment. I tossed my bag on the table, and just like the other day, I left my boots and coat on the floor because I didn't care. "But I'm so worked up that I don't want to fight. I need you more than I want to push you away." When I got all the heavy layers off my body, I moved into his chest and closed my eyes. His body was hard as concrete, not soft like the pillows on his bed. My arms wrapped around him, and I took comfort in the man that I loved, even though he'd lied to me.

Bosco wrapped his arms around me and rested his chin on the top of my head. "Didn't go well, I take it?"

He was so warm, searing hot against my cheek. "It went as well as I expected it to go."

His hand moved under the fall of my hair and to the back of my neck. He gently massaged the area as his other arm circled my waist and held me close. He didn't address why I was pissed off at him, probably because he'd figured it out on his own.

I pulled away and looked into his pretty eyes. He was the most powerful man I knew, but even he didn't have the power to fix this.

"Are you going to let me explain myself?" He slid

his hands into the pockets of his sweatpants as he tilted his head slightly to look at me.

I felt betrayed that he'd kept this secret from me for over a month. The entire time I was stressing about my father's reaction, Bosco knew exactly what that reaction would be. He kept quiet, hiding it as a dirty secret. Nearly every person involved had all the facts, but I didn't know anything. "No."

He maintained the same stoic expression.

"I just want to go to bed and forget about this until morning." I was emotionally drained from the intense conversation with my father. None of it had unfolded the way I wanted. I couldn't even anticipate the conversation because he dropped a bomb on me the second I walked inside. Bosco could have at least told me the truth before I faced my father for the discussion.

"Will I be joining you?"

"Yes." I walked into his bedroom and shucked the rest of my clothes, leaving my panties on and fishing a t-shirt out of his drawer. I pulled it on then got into bed.

Bosco joined me a moment later, lying beside me in his boxers. He cradled me to his chest, and we lay there in the darkness, even though it was barely five.

I'd skipped lunch and dinner, but I still wasn't hungry. I just wanted to lie there and think about nothing.

He dragged his fingers lightly down my back and pressed a kiss to my hairline. "I love you, Beautiful."

I wasn't ready to be angry with him, so I put my

feelings on hold and let him comfort me. "I love you too…"

W HEN I WOKE UP THE NEXT MORNING, MY FURY WAS at the forefront.

Bosco noticed my anger in my movements, the way I quickly got ready for work without looking at him twice. He watched me hurry to do my hair and makeup and pull on my clothes before I marched for the door. "So…now, you're officially mad?" He followed behind me, his hands moving into the pockets of his sweatpants.

"Very." I hit the code on the elevator, and the doors opened. "We'll talk about this when I get home."

"Why don't we talk about it now?" He grabbed me by the elbow and gently tugged me back toward him.

"Because I have to work. I already closed the shop enough times trying to talk to my father. I can't miss any more time." I looked at him, the fire smoldering in my eyes. "And it would have been helpful to know he was avoiding me on purpose. Wouldn't have wasted so much of my time." I yanked my arm out of his grasp and stepped into the elevator.

Bosco let me go, but he didn't look happy about it. He slid his hands into his pockets as he stared at me, holding my gaze as the doors slowly closed and hid him from view.

The elevator descended to the lobby, and I kept picturing Bosco's face in my mind. Handsome, apologetic, and full of angst. I could tell he wanted to yank me back into the penthouse and not let me go until he'd earned my forgiveness.

That was how I was sure he knew he was wrong for what he did.

I got into the back seat of the car, and his men dropped me off at work. I hardly ever drove my car anymore, only when I went to visit my family because it would be hostile to show up with a dozen armed guards on their property.

I arrived at the shop and got to work, doing my best not to think about all the drama going on in my life. My father and boyfriend were more aware of the situation than me—the person connecting them together.

I felt so stupid.

This entire time, Bosco had known my father hated him. And my father knew about Bosco too. Even Griffin was aware of everything, and he never once mentioned it to me. Did Vanessa know as well?

Who could I trust?

Around lunchtime, I got a special visitor.

My mom.

"Carmen." Mom appeared at the counter, sneaking up on me slightly. She smiled at me like she wasn't angry, just happy to see her daughter.

My heart nearly jumped out of my chest, especially because I knew exactly why she was there. The storm that had hit our family was spinning at full force, and there was no way to escape. Even when I stood in the eye, I could feel the wind swirl around me. "Hey, Mama." I finally found a smile when I recovered from the shock. "Sorry, you snuck up on me."

"I walked straight at you," she said. "You were even looking at me."

"Sorry…my mind was elsewhere."

Her smile started to fall. "Your father told me what happened, Carmen…" She rested her arms on the counter as she looked at me, her fingers interlocked together. "He's still fairly angry about it. I've been trying to talk him down. I think I'll need a few more days to make a dent in his armor."

"Well, thanks for trying."

"Is this the same man you mentioned a few months ago?"

I nodded.

"The one who isn't right for you but you can't stay away from?"

"Yeah."

"Why do you think he's not right for you?"

"In the beginning, I thought he was too dangerous. But now I know he's completely harmless to me. When I realized he was a good man, I knew Father would be my next obstacle. After talking with him…it doesn't seem likely there will be any success."

My mom tucked her brown hair behind her ear, her mocha eyes glowing beautifully. I inherited all my good looks from her, only getting my father's eyes and subtle hints of his Barsetti blood. My skin wasn't as dark as Vanessa's because I took after my mother so much. "This is the man you want to spend the rest of your life with?"

Bosco told me he would give me whatever I wanted. Because of that, there was no doubt in my mind. He loved me enough to sacrifice everything, to walk away from all that he'd built just to have me. If that wasn't love, I didn't know what was. "Yes." The idea of finding someone new and forcing myself to love him the way I loved Bosco sounded awful. "He's the one."

"You're sure?" Mom asked.

I nodded. "Absolutely."

She rested her hand on mine and gave me a gentle pat. "Then I accept him, Carmen. In time, I'm sure I'll like him. But since I haven't even met him, that's kinda hard for me to do right this second."

That was surprisingly kind, even though my mom had always done everything for me. "Thank you."

"Your father told me Bosco is one of the biggest crime lords in the city. He's a bit arrogant. He set his eyes on you then never stopped pursuing you. Your father said you tried to break things off with him, but Bosco wouldn't let you."

"Yes...not his finest qualities." I didn't want to lie to my parents about my past with Bosco. I wasn't ashamed of it because we grew into something more. That felt so long ago that it didn't seem relevant anymore. "But that's not who he is anymore. He's…extremely kind. All he cares about is protecting me. He would die before he let anything happen to me. So instead of focusing on those moments, focus on that."

My mother nodded, giving a slight smile. "I believe you, Carmen. I'll keep an open mind…and I'll try to convince your father he should do the same. The only reason it's difficult for him is because he's spent his entire life protecting you, and he can't stop that impulse. He feels like he needs to save you…even though you don't need saving. He loves you so much that he's always imagined some Prince Charming riding in on a white horse. Your prince comes from a good family, he's rich, and he's squeaky clean. Since this doesn't match your father's expectations, he's disappointed—not because he's not getting what he wants, but because you aren't getting what he wants."

"I understand…but I don't want Prince Charming."

"I know," she said. "Trust me, I do. Good men are boring, if you ask me. Women want a man who's real, who has dimensions and layers. They want a man who pushes the boundaries and isn't afraid to get his hands dirty. You would never be happy with some…accountant, doctor, or lawyer."

I couldn't picture Bosco with a regular job like that.

"The fact that Bosco had the talent to accomplish what he has at such a young age is admirable," my mother said. "Maybe he was motivated by greed, but for someone to pull that together and retain his power and esteem for so long is incredible. Only a very powerful man would have been able to pull off something like that. His success is so incredible that even your father and uncle are intimidated by it…and that's saying something."

Sometimes I forgot that my mother was so much cooler than my father. She was more pragmatic and logical when she viewed the world. There was never pride or emotion in her decisions, just objectivity. She could immediately see past Bosco's faults and highlight his charms. "Thanks for having such an open mind."

"Well, your father is extremely biased in how he views things. Sometimes he forgets he wasn't always the man he is now. Once upon a time, he wasn't so different from Bosco. He was young, greedy, and hotheaded. He thought he could do whatever he wanted without retribution. But then he met a special woman, and that changed his path permanently. It made him reevaluate what kind of man he wanted to be. He abandoned the darkness and embraced the light, finally finding a reason to become a good man."

I smiled. "Was that special woman you, Mama?"

"Yes." She patted my hand. "I've done my best to remind your father of that, but it doesn't change the way he feels. He thinks you deserve better than I did. He loves you so much he can't see straight. You have every right to be frustrated with him, but don't forget, he's only behaving this way because he loves you so damn much."

"I know…"

"I'll make him cut you and Bosco some slack. But I ask you to do the same for him."

I nodded. "I'll always cut Father some slack. He's earned it."

———

AFTER TALKING WITH MY MOTHER, I WASN'T AS stressed about the situation as I was before. Now that I had one parent on my side, it would only be a matter of time before the other caved. My mother was naturally persuasive, having the ability to change anyone's mind about anything. Hopefully, changing my father's mind would be simple.

When I took the elevator to the penthouse and saw Bosco standing right in the living room, my previous anger came back to me. The man I slept with every single night had betrayed me. He'd carried on the lie for weeks, choosing to withhold vital information that would have changed everything.

"Still mad, huh?" he asked, standing in his gray sweatpants.

"Yep." I set my purse down and shed my coat.

"Alright." He took a deep breath as he waited for me to start yelling.

I faced him and crossed my arms over my chest. That handsome face couldn't bring my rage to a smolder, not this time. It didn't matter how pretty his blue eyes were, how masculine that jawline was. "You lied to me. You made me look like a fool. You kept a secret from me for over a month. How could you possibly justify that?"

"It's simple." He spoke to me the same way he spoke to his men when he was at the casino, holding in all his emotion and talking to me like he didn't feel a thing. All he felt was authority and power. "Your father made a mistake marching onto my turf like that. If he weren't your father, he would have been thrown in the ring. I would have made him fight his own brother and watched every hit until the end. He threatened me on my own property, and then he insulted me by trying to buy me off with a hundred million dollars—which is pennies to me. I told him I would do him a favor by not telling you what happened—because it made your father look like an ass. I told him we weren't just fucking, that we loved each other. I looked him in the eye and told him I would die for you—in a heartbeat. Based on all the mercy I showed, I think he believed me. I didn't think he would confess to his crimes, not when it made him look so selfish. But I guess your father isn't as much of a coward as I thought he was."

It was a legitimate explanation, but I was still angry. "This whole time you knew…"

"I would have told you, but I couldn't do that without compromising him. Even if your father and I have our disagreements, I don't want to affect your relationship with him. As a man with no parents, I understand how important it is to cherish them while you can. I never want to come between you and your father. I just want to be accepted among you."

"There's nothing my father could ever do to make me stop loving him, to make me turn my back on him. I was pissed when he told me what he did, because it was wrong, but I know he only did it because he loves me. I forgave him for it."

"As you should," he said. "He meant well...even if his actions were idiotic. I respect a man who protects the women he loves. He and I are the same in that regard...even if he doesn't realize it."

"He will realize it...in time."

He watched me for a long while, his eyes boring into mine. "If you forgive him, then you must forgive me."

"Of course I do. But I'm still mad at him, and I'm still mad at you."

He bowed his head slightly.

"I feel so stupid going down there without knowing. This entire time, my father knew about you, and I was assuming otherwise. Now I understand he was avoiding me because he didn't want to address the truth. It's just...embarrassing."

"Nothing to be embarrassed about," he said calmly. "He should be embarrassed for blowing you off like that."

"I guess he wasn't ready to deal with this."

"No. He's had a hard time."

I kept my arms crossed over my chest, my teeth

grinding together in annoyance. "I'm irritated that this is my personal life, yet everyone knows more about it than I do. People are sneaking around behind my back and leaving me in the cold. Even Griffin was doing it."

"Griffin was in a tough spot, in his defense."

"Are you seriously defending him?" I asked, an eyebrow raised.

"It's not black and white, Beautiful. That's all I'm saying. Since everything is done and we're still standing here, maybe you should let this go."

"Easy for you to say…"

"The worst is over. Let's enjoy our small victory."

I couldn't handle any more lies, any more half-truths. Griffin didn't owe me anything, and I didn't expect more out of my father, but I expected more out of the man I loved. "I never want this to happen again. If you want to be my man, that means no more secrets. I'm serious."

Bosco stared at me as he considered the question, standing a short distance away from me with his hands in his pockets. "Alright."

"Is that a promise?"

He nodded. "That's a promise. I'll never keep anything from you again. But remember, that's a double-edged sword."

"I'll take my chances. If this is gonna last a lifetime, then I want a partner I can trust, someone I can count on. I want to be in the loop, not oblivious to important knowledge that's been shared right under my nose."

That wasn't much to ask for, so I didn't feel out of line. He'd already sacrificed plenty for me, but I wanted a little more.

"Alright."

Now that I'd gotten what I wanted, I kept my arms crossed over my chest, unsure what to do next.

"Can I kiss you now?" The corner of his mouth rose in a lopsided grin.

I loved that smile and couldn't resist it. "Yes…"

He moved into me and bent his neck down to kiss me on the mouth, his scruff rubbing against me slightly. His lips were soft, but his jaw was hard. He lightly sucked my bottom lip into his mouth before he let go.

"So your mom stopped by?" He knew everything about my life, even as it was unfolding. "And how did that go?"

"My mom is a lot more logical than my father. She said if you're the man I want to spend the rest of my life with, then she accepts that. She trusts my decision and supports it. But she needs to get to know you before she can actually like you."

"Wow. She's way better than your father."

I chuckled. "Yeah, she's great. She's a lot more understanding. Doesn't have unrealistic expectations of anything."

"I look forward to meeting her…whenever that time comes."

"I'm not sure when it'll happen. She said she's still

working on getting my father to see reason. She'll need a few more days."

"The fact that she thinks she can do it in days instead of years is impressive."

"Well, my mom can do amazing things. She's a superhero."

His smile faded slightly, and a note of sadness entered his look.

Somehow, I knew he was thinking about his own mother, the woman he respected most in the world. He still missed her, even though he was a grown man who didn't need anyone for anything. "I'm sorry…"

"It's okay," he said quietly. "Sometimes the sadness just hits me, and it takes me a second to recover. I still miss her. Your mother reminds me of her…at least, based on the way you describe her."

"They are alike. They are both women who don't put up with bullshit."

"Yeah…and you're like that too." His hands squeezed my hips. "One of the reasons I fell in love with you."

17

BOSCO

AFTER A FEW DAYS HAD PASSED, Carmen forgot about her anger entirely.

Our nights were spent naked under the sheets, and our afternoons were filled with quiet conversations over dinner then time on the couch in front of the TV. It was still unclear what would happen with her father, but when he was ready to face me, he would have to make his first move.

A week later, it happened.

We were sitting on the couch together when his name popped up on Carmen's phone screen.

She held the phone up to her face. "It's my father…" The screen was clearly visible to me, but she said it out loud anyway, like she was saying it to herself. She took the call and pressed the phone to her ear. "Hey, Father."

"Hey, sweetheart." His tone didn't seem threatening,

but it wasn't full of fatherly love either. "Hope I'm not calling at a bad time."

"No, we're just watching TV." She grimaced slightly when she mentioned me, like that was a stupid mistake.

He would have to get used to it. We lived together now, and she wasn't going back to her apartment unless she was packing up the rest of her stuff and vacating it.

He didn't address what she'd said. "Your mother and I have been talking a lot lately…"

"Yeah, she told me she would wear you down, dent your armor a bit."

"And she finally has…because she doesn't let up."

Carmen smiled. "She gets what she wants, Father. That's why you fell in love with her in the first place."

He chuckled slightly. "Yeah…I admire her perseverance. Anyway…maybe the four of us could have dinner over here tomorrow. Your mother will cook, and we'll have some wine…and talk." He'd invited both of us to dinner, but he struggled to get the words out nonetheless. He hated every second of this…but at least he was trying.

"We would love to. And thanks for inviting us." Carmen's happiness was obvious, both in her voice and on her face. This was what she wanted, the beginning of progress.

I admired him for making the call himself. He could have had his wife do it, but he did it personally.

He paused for a long time. "See you then, sweetheart." Then he hung up.

Carmen set the phone down and looked at me. "I guess we have plans tomorrow night."

"Yeah, I guess we do." I wasn't thrilled about spending time with her father, but since this was important to her and necessary to our relationship, I would do it—and be as polite as possible.

"I think everything is going to be okay. Since my mom is on board, it's only a matter of time before my father relaxes. We just need to be patient. If he insults you or anything…just let it go."

I turned to her, my smile disappearing. "Beautiful, I love you. But I don't let any man insult me. It's one of the reasons you love me. I'm not going to change who I am. I promise I won't provoke him, but I'll certainly defend myself if necessary." I would compromise with her on anything, but not that. He'd already called me an asshole a few times at the casino, but I didn't rise to his rage. It would have been easy for me to let my pride get to me and shoot him between the eyes, but I didn't. I gave him a grace period since it was our first meeting. But there would be no more mercy from me.

Carmen didn't try to talk me out of it. "Alright. Fair enough."

I DROVE THE BUGATTI OUT OF FLORENCE AND INTO the countryside. Since this was a family dinner, bringing two dozen guards wouldn't make a very good impression. It was his property, so I didn't have any jurisdiction.

The men followed me until I was two minutes from the house. Then they set up a perimeter in a two-mile radius of the property, securing everything around the house other than the property itself.

Cane would never know.

"Here." Carmen pointed to the two-story house surrounded by the limestone wall. "That's their place."

The gate had been left open, so I drove up the path until I came to a roundabout with a statue of a horse in the center. Water was flowing from the fountain, creating a serene backdrop that complemented the lush landscape.

I wasn't nervous whatsoever. I didn't get nervous. But I wanted this to be over so we could go home. I preferred solitude with Carmen, sharing my space with only her alone. I lived for the nights when she walked around in my t-shirt, no panties underneath. I lived for the moments when she fell asleep on the couch while her head rested on my thigh. I lived for the moments when she was underneath me in bed, coming around my dick several times in a single go. It was easy to please a woman who wanted to be satisfied so thoroughly.

I locked the car then we walked up to the front door.

"This should be fun..." Carmen spoke under her breath, showing her restless nerves.

"The fact that he's invited me to his home is a big step. That's the biggest gesture of a truce."

"Yeah…that's a good point."

The door opened, revealing Carmen's mom. She wore a long-sleeved red dress with tights underneath. She had the same brown hair Carmen possessed, but different colored eyes. I saw so many similarities that they seemed more like sisters than mother and daughter.

She hugged Carmen tightly before she turned to me. "Please come in, Bosco. I'm Adelina." Instead of giving me a handshake, she wrapped her arms around me and hugged me the way she'd hugged her daughter.

The way my mother used to hug me.

She rubbed my back before she pulled away. "It's so nice to meet you. Can I take your coat?"

"It's lovely to meet you as well, Mrs. Barsetti." I stripped off my coat. "And thank you."

She hung it on the coatrack before she turned back to me. "Please call me Adelina. There are so many Mrs. Barsettis now that it's just confusing. I share that name with three other women."

I chuckled. "That is a lot."

Adelina pulled Carmen to her side and kissed her on the temple. "You look beautiful, honey. I like this sweater."

"Thanks, Mama," Carmen said, hugging her mother back.

I already adored Adelina far more than Cane. I

wasn't even sure how a cold man like Cane landed such a warm wife.

"Your father is setting the table in the dining room. Let's join him." She walked with me beside her. "Red or white wine, Bosco?"

"I like both," I answered. "So whatever Carmen is having."

"Her favorite is red." Adelina guided us to the dining room.

Cane was there, the table set and a decanter of scotch open in the middle. His short glass was empty because he'd started drinking long before we got there. He didn't look at me. He looked at his daughter first and gave her a smile that was so forced it look odd. He hugged her and kissed her on the temple. "Hey, sweetheart. Thanks for coming over."

"We're glad to be here." Carmen stepped away then darted her eyes back and forth between us, noticing the tension as the two of us stared at each other.

Cane looked at me, but no hand was extended. He seemed to retain his calmness until he actually had to make eye contact with me. Now that we were looking directly at one another, all of his courage seemed to evaporate—replaced by the same anger he showed me the last time we met.

I didn't want to put up with his hypocritical bullshit, but I knew it would mean the world to Carmen if we could work this out. I wanted this woman more than anything, and I was going to do anything to keep her—

even swallow my pride and make the first gesture. "Thank you for inviting me to dinner, Mr. Barsetti." I extended my right hand to shake his.

Cane didn't even look at it.

Carmen sighed under her breath, but it was so quiet in the room that we could all hear it.

Cane couldn't bring himself to do it, still seeing me as the enemy. He turned away and approached the table. "I'm glad you could join us, Bosco." His tone was ice-cold, like he didn't mean a word he said.

Adelina watched him with daggers of disappoint-ment in her eyes. "Ignore him, Bosco." She said it loud enough so Cane could hear. "He'll come around. Have a seat, and we'll get started."

I wasn't offended by his aloofness, but I knew his frosty greeting would rip Carmen apart. I pulled out the chair for her like I always did and then sat down.

Cane watched my movements. "I'm not impressed by your little show."

Carmen glared at her father.

I unfolded the napkin and placed it in my lap. "I don't care what you think, Mr. Barsetti. I pull out the chair for Carmen everywhere we go because she's my lady, and I put my lady first. How else would you explain my visit here tonight? I'm one of the richest men in the country, so I could be doing absolutely anything else in the world right now. But I'm here—with you. I understand this is hard for you, sir. But your coldness doesn't hurt me. It hurts Carmen." I grabbed the bottle of wine and filled her glass before I filled mine.

Cane stared at me with the same hostile glare, not saying a word but conveying all his feelings and thoughts in just his expression. "Arrogant. Pompous. Asshole."

Adelina shook her head slightly. "Oh dear. We haven't even served the food, and you're acting like wolves."

Cane repeated the words he'd just said, but this time slower. "Arrogant. Pompous. Asshole."

Carmen sighed beside me, covering half of her face with her fingers.

"Yes, I'm all those things," I said in agreement. "But not when it comes to Carmen."

"But you have no problem acting like an asshole in my house." Cane's voice rose higher, his anger bouncing off the vaulted ceiling.

"Cane." Adelina silenced him with her stern voice. "He literally just sat down, and you're already ripping into him."

"What happened to giving him a chance?" Carmen demanded.

"He just behaved like a jerk." Cane addressed his daughter next, throwing me under the bus.

"Because you provoked him," Carmen countered. "Father, you need to calm down. You're being ridiculous right now."

I was glad she defended me instead of letting her father get away with his juvenile behavior.

"Let's start over," I offered. "Let's just forget the last two minutes ever happened."

Adelina looked at me. "I think that's a very forgiving offer, Bosco. And we all accept."

"I don't," Cane barked. "You think you're a better man than me? Try being a father to a wonderful daughter. Then we'll see how forgiving you really are."

This man couldn't even look at me without losing his shit. Just my face alone made him spiral out of control. When he spoke to Carmen last night, he'd seemed reasonably calm. But now that I sat across from him, calm simply wasn't possible. I tried another tactic, only because I loved Carmen so damn much. "I'll have dinner with you as many times as it takes to gain your acceptance. I'll put up with your rage and your bullshit as long as you want. Nothing you say is gonna chase me off. It doesn't matter how insufferable you are, I'll put up with it. I love your daughter, and I'm here for the long-haul, the forever, the rest of my life kind of commitment. You're the most important man in her life, so I'll keep sitting here as many times as it takes for you to give me a chance. Just to be clear, I don't care if you don't like me. But it would mean the world to your daughter, the woman I love, if we could at least try to move forward. I'm willing to keep an open mind if you are."

He held my gaze without blinking, respecting my speech but also hating me more because of it.

The corner of Adelina's mouth rose in a slight smile.

Carmen didn't do anything. She just waited for some kind of reaction.

Cane kept up the stare. It seemed like he could do it forever.

"I promised Carmen I would sell the casino to my brother, completely cutting ties to the business so I could live in Tuscany with her. She wants a family, and I've agreed to give her that. Even after selling the casino, my net worth is astronomical. I can give her the life she wants, the kind of life no other man could offer her. You think I'm not good enough for your daughter, but you're wrong. I'm the best candidate for the job. Maybe I'm pompous. Maybe I'm arrogant. But you should want an arrogant man. If he has so much success that he is arrogant, then he understands his self-worth. I don't put up with bullshit—not even from you. That's the kind of man you want for your daughter, someone who doesn't bow down to anyone. The only person I've ever kneeled for is your daughter—and that's exactly how it should be."

Cane remained silent.

Adelina grinned widely.

Carmen still didn't say anything.

"Well, I like him," Adelina said. "I think he's a confident young man who fights for what he wants. He's given up everything for our daughter, and that's more than enough proof for me."

Cane broke his trance and looked at his wife. "You remember what he did. You remember who this man is, what he's done—"

"And that has no bearing on the man I'm looking at now." She stood up to her husband the way Carmen stood up to me. "I see a man who loves and respects our daughter, who's willing to do anything for her, even put up with you. If he stands up to you, that means he's always going to stand up for our daughter. That's more important to me than who he used to be. And you should be the last person to judge a man for something like that." She turned away and drank her wine.

Cane didn't challenge her again. He slowly turned his head back to me, the fury not so apparent in his gaze. "I won't apologize for what I said. I won't apologize for wanting the best for my daughter. But…I will try to be better."

That was better than nothing, I guess.

THE WOMEN DID THE DISHES IN THE KITCHEN, SO I sat on the other couch while Cane sat across from me. Like a baby with a security blanket, he brought his decanter of scotch everywhere he went in the house. Now it was on the table between us.

I helped myself to a glass, enclosed in a private

space with him without the women to mitigate the tension. "I bought a place down the road from here. It's within two miles. Three stories. Five bedrooms—"

"Are you trying to be a show-off right now?" He interrupted me, his gaze as cold as it was earlier.

"No." I swallowed the harsh retort I wanted to throw back at him. "I bought it for Carmen and me… whenever we get through this nightmare. She wants to live close to you while she raises a family. I just wanted you to know I'm not trying to take her away from you."

He stared at the fire burning in the fireplace.

"I thought that might make you happy."

"The idea of you shacking up with my daughter doesn't make me happy at all, Bosco. I wish you'd never met her."

This guy was the stubbornest person on the planet. And that was saying something because I was pretty stubborn. "That's a shame because my mother would have loved Carmen. It breaks my heart that they never met."

The mention of my dead mother seemed to soften Cane, or at least made him rethink being such an asshole. "What about your father?"

"Abandoned us after my brother was born." I didn't feel any pain about it. I never sensed like there something missing in my life. My mother raised me to be a man—and she did a great job.

"You never spoke to him again?"

"No. And I'm glad I didn't. If he ever came back

into my life, I would tell him to fuck off. I don't harbor a grudge against him because my brother and I didn't have a father. My mother was more than enough. But I'll always hate him for abandoning her, making her work two jobs just to support us. Raising two kids as a single mom is tough work. His behavior was unforgivable."

Cane stared at me.

"I think that's why I fell for Carmen so easily. She's strong the way my mother was, independent, smart, and fierce. Most women want me for my money, but Carmen couldn't care less. She can do anything she wants on her own. She doesn't need a man. But that makes me want to be the man she never needed in the first place." I wasn't sure why I was saying all of this to Cane. I guess I wanted to have a conversation that didn't have anything to do with the casino. The one subject we had in common was Carmen. "I like taking care of her…" She let me buy her diamonds that she never asked for. She let me protect her with my army of men. She let me buy her dresses that she loved. She let me share my home with her. She wasn't the kind of woman to be dependent on a man, but she let herself be dependent on me.

Cane looked away. "I know you love her. You don't need to keep trying to convince me."

"Then what's the problem?"

"If any man said he loved my daughter, I would believe him. She's the most wonderful woman on this planet. She's beautiful, smart, ambitious…knows how to throw an awesome right hook. We both know she could have any man she wants."

"Then why is this so hard for you to accept? I have all the money in the world, all the resources. I want to give Carmen everything. For once in my life, I don't want to be greedy and keep all my money to myself. I want to give that woman the world."

"Bosco." He turned his body toward me and held his glass in his fingers. "It's nothing personal. You come from the underworld. I just don't want my daughter to marry someone from that world. I spent decades trying to get out of it, but it still keeps pulling me back in."

"I'm not part of the underworld," I said confidently. "I own it. I can make any problem go away."

"And every man hates you for it. You might have the respect of most men, but you have the envy of even more. There's nothing an unhappy man wants more than to destroy a happy man's life. You'll always be a target."

"My brother is taking over the casino."

"And you're associated with him. If people want to get to Ronan, they'll come after you."

He had me there. "I'm very cautious. I have fifty men who have secured a two-mile perimeter around your property."

"And I'm aware of their presence—because I'm cautious too."

Now I stared at him with tension rising in my chest.

"The worst feature of a man is arrogance, not because it's tacky, but because he thinks he's invincible. And that's when his enemies find his weakness—because he's too conceited to think he has any." He pointed his glass at me. "That's what I see when I look at you. I know my daughter loves you and you love her, but that's not always enough. The best way to be safe is to disappear. My brother and I have been trying to disappear for decades, but our sons have inherited our affinity for trouble."

At the root of all his anxiety was fear. He just wanted his daughter to be safe. "Cane, I can't promise that nothing will ever happen to her, because that's just not a realistic promise to make. But I can promise you that I will always protect her, and I will do everything in my power to keep her safe. If it ever came down to it, I would take a bullet for her. I would sacrifice my life for hers."

He held my gaze as he absorbed my words.

"That's the best I can do. That's the best you can do."

"But I'm afraid she's in more danger by being with you. Surely, you must agree."

She was kidnapped in an alleyway, and that had nothing to do with me. But The Butcher became obsessed with her when he spotted us together. In both cases, I fixed the problem, just as I did in the bank. "She's also just as likely to be hurt in some other way. At least with me, she has all the protection money can buy."

"Money can't buy everything, Bosco. It can't buy peace."

———

AFTER WE SAID GOOD NIGHT, WE GOT INTO MY CAR and drove back to Florence.

Carmen sighed in the seat beside me, her gaze focused out the window into the darkness surrounding us. "I'm sorry my father was so difficult."

"It's alright, Carmen. Not your fault."

"I don't know if he's ever going to be okay with this…"

He would have to be, even if I had to force him. "We'll figure it out, Beautiful." I held her hand on the center console.

"What did you guys talk about when we were doing the dishes? I didn't hear any yelling."

"Same old shit. I told him I loved you. He said that wasn't enough."

"Then what is enough?" she asked.

"He's just scared that you're going to get hurt because of me, because of my tenure at the casino. I understand his concern because he's just protective and wants to make sure nothing happens to you. But what he doesn't understand is you're in danger no matter who you're with. At least with me, I can save you."

"That's a good point. Did you say that to him?"

"Yes."

"And?"

I shook my head. "I don't think he's gonna change his mind."

She sighed. "He will in time. I'll make him change his mind, or my mother will. If my mom is on board with this, then he should be too."

"I love your mom, by the way. She's pretty amazing."

Carmen smiled. "I love her too. She really balances out my father, erases his intensity."

It reminded me of Carmen, how she balanced out my flaws with her endless good qualities. I squeezed her hand before I brought it to my lips for a kiss. "We'll get through this—together. Because I'm not giving up on you, Carmen. I'm not gonna stop until you're Carmen Roth."

"Carmen Roth…" She stared at our joined hands as a small smile stretched across her mouth. "I like that."

18

CARMEN

I WALKED inside the gallery and approached Vanessa from behind.

Her bodyguard watched me like a hawk.

"Vanessa."

My cousin turned around at the stern tone in my voice. "Yes? Something wrong?" She'd just finished placing a new painting on the hook, another Barsetti masterpiece that would fetch hundreds of euros. She'd become so popular in the city that her prices were steadily rising. "Griffin told me your dinner last night didn't go too well."

"That sounds about right…since Griffin knows everything about my personal life." I crossed my arms over my chest.

She grabbed both of my wrists and pinned them down to my sides. "Okay, enough with the attitude. What's your problem?"

"My problem is that Griffin told my father about Bosco weeks ago, and neither one of you told me. After everything I did for you guys in the beginning, this is how you repay me? I felt like an idiot when my father said he already knew."

Judging by the bewilderment in Vanessa's gaze, she genuinely had no idea. "Griffin never told me he told your father. He kept that a secret from me too. I'm just finding out about this now."

Vanessa would never lie about anything, so I believed her. "Oh...then I apologize."

"Damn right. I would never betray you. You know that. That's probably why Griffin never told me— because I would betray him quicker than I would betray you."

When she said that, my shoulders relaxed, and I felt a smile emerge. "You're right...I'm sorry."

"So, if your father already knew, then that must mean the interrogation was a little easier. You know, since he wasn't caught by surprise."

"You would think...but, no. We went to dinner there last night, and my father turned into an asshole."

She shook her head. "Just like my father..."

"I'm not seventeen. I'm twenty-five. My father needs to dial it down...but I don't think he can."

"It took six months for my father to come around. Just the fact that your father invited Bosco over for dinner is a drastic improvement to what I experienced. So that's something to be thankful for."

"I guess…"

"Our fathers are just overprotective. Nothing is ever gonna change that."

"You're right."

She patted me on the shoulder. "At least Bosco is willing to put up with it. He could just find someone else if he didn't love you so much. Watching a man fight for you like that is actually pretty sexy."

Watching my father and Bosco rip out each other's throats was not sexy. I just wanted them to get along. "I want what Griffin and your father have now. I want Bosco and my father to respect each other and like each other. Bosco and I aren't getting married tomorrow, but I would like to know that possibility is in our future. I like the idea of living down the road from them with our four children."

She rubbed her stomach. "I still can't believe you want to have four of these. I'm not even finished with one, and I'm telling you, it's no picnic. You're hungry all the time, nauseous all the time, your clothes don't fit anymore—"

"Your husband wants to have sex with you all the time, wait on you hand and food, and gets even more protective because he loves both of you? No, that sounds like exactly what I want."

Her hand stilled on her stomach, and she smiled. "Yeah…that part is pretty great."

I always knew I wanted to be a mom. It was more important to me than my shop and anything else I wanted to do with my life. Having a big house filled with kids sounded perfect to me. I had two cousins and one brother, and having four kids would make that tradition continue.

"Just keep holding on," Vanessa said. "Something's gotta give eventually. Your father will cave. You can't fight love with hate. It's just not possible."

"I hope you're right...because Bosco is the one."

She gave me that soft smile she only showed once in a great while. It was reserved for the people she was closest to, an intimate look outsiders rarely got to see. "Then giving up isn't an option, Carmen. You fight for him until you win."

19

CARTER

I MADE a snack for Luca when he came home from school, and we sat together at the kitchen table doing his math homework. Math was his worst subject, while reading was his greatest, but since engineering was completely based on math, it was my strongest talent. I walked through the steps and did the best I could to teach him—not do it for him.

He was halfway done with the sheet when he lost interest. "Can I watch TV now?"

"Are you done with your homework?"

"No…"

"Then, no." I liked being a father to Luca because he was a great kid who took after his mother. He had so many of her features, and that made me love him the second I laid eyes on him. His heart was just like hers, strong and full of forgiveness. But times like these, when

I had to discipline him and be the bad guy, weren't the moments I loved the most.

He rolled his eyes.

"Luca." I gave him my stern tone. "Don't roll your eyes at me."

"We've been at it for an hour."

"And we would be done by now if you concentrated. The sooner we're finished, the sooner we can do something else. Trust me, I don't want to do this either. Now, try again." I pressed my finger against the sheet, hitting the problem that he needed to start. "Think about everything we went over. You should be able to do this one."

Luca didn't roll his eyes again, but he sighed loudly. "Whatever…" He started working out the problem with his pencil.

I watched his work, pleased that he was doing it right. When I gave him some tough love, he got his act together and concentrated. Fortunately, I've never had to discipline him for anything worse because he was a good kid. All Mia had to do was whistle twice, and he got his act together.

She was a good mom.

And that made being a stepfather a lot easier, especially since I hadn't known anything about kids until Luca came into my life.

The sound of the opening garage reached my ears, and I knew it was Mia. She'd gone to the grocery store to pick up a few things, and I picked up Luca from school.

"Keep working on that while I help your mom unload the car."

"Alright." His pencil kept scratching away.

I went outside and watched Mia open the back end of the SUV. "Hey, sweetheart." My chest filled with happiness any time I saw her. Even though I'd seen her that morning, it seemed like it'd been a lifetime.

Her eyes mirrored mine. "Back at you."

My arms circled her waist, and I kissed her in the garage, kissing her hard because our son was inside and couldn't see us. I backed her up against the bumper and dug my hands into her hair.

She kissed me back with the same desire, wanting more now from her husband than she did when I was just her love. Her diamond ring was on her left hand where it always stayed. I never took mine off either. "You missed me or what?" she said against my mouth.

I pressed my erection against her stomach. "You can't tell?"

She chuckled. "Oh yes, I can tell."

"Mom?"

I broke apart from her right away, embarrassed Luca had caught us in the act.

His voice came from the front of the car, so he probably hadn't caught the details of our embrace. "Did you get me those candies I like?" He came around the bumper, seemingly oblivious to what was just happening.

I grabbed two of the grocery bags and pretended nothing had transpired in the first place.

"Depends," she said. "Is your homework done?"

Luca dropped his head in sadness. "Mom!"

"Finish your homework, and I'll give them to you. But I also got you another treat." She ran her fingers through his hair. "Because I know you've been working so hard to bring up your math grade, and I'm proud of you for not giving up."

Luca lifted his head again. "What is it?"

"You'll have to wait and see. Show me your homework when you're finished."

"Alright!" Luca ran back into the house.

I turned back to Mia. "You're so good with him."

"He's a sweetheart, so it's pretty easy."

"I think he's a sweetheart because you're a sweetheart." I gave her a quick kiss on the mouth then walked away.

I WAS IN MY OFFICE WHEN LUCA CAME INSIDE. "DAD?"

"Hmm?" I looked up from the schematic I was examining, the dimensions of the new car we were sending to the factories.

Luca stood in the doorway. "Mom says dinner is ready."

I'd gotten used to hearing him call me dad, but it still filled my heart with warmth every time he said it. I'd grown to love that little boy like he'd always been mine, like that other asshole had never existed in the first place. Sometimes I felt bad for the guy…because he missed out on the most amazing kid in the world. "I'll be right down, little man."

"Alright." Luca shut the door and left, running down the hallway to the stairs.

I turned back to my paperwork to make my final notes.

Then my phone began to ring.

It was the last name I expected to see on the screen, the very last person in the world I was thinking about. I pictured his blue eyes, stern features, and the Russian accent that emerged from that harsh mouth before he even spoke.

Egor.

Frozen to the spot, I didn't know what to do.

It kept ringing.

Why would he call me after all this time? Mia had been mine for over a year now. Was he still thinking about her? Did he spot her in town somewhere? Or did he want to discuss something else entirely?

I wanted to ignore the call, but I would be haunted by curiosity. I'd rather face him and know what he wanted than wonder if my family was in trouble. I cleared my throat and took the call. "Long time, no speak." I kept it casual, like I still had nothing to hide from this man.

"Too long."

I waited in silence over the phone, waiting to see what he wanted without giving myself away. I had to be casual, indifferent. After all, I had nothing to hide…at least, that was how we'd left it.

When I didn't speak again, he did. "I wanted to catch up, Carter. How have you been?"

The strangeness of the conversation told me my worst fear had come true. There was no other explanation for his random call. When we spoke before, he always got straight to the point because he was a busy man. "Busy. You?"

He chuckled. "Yes, I know you've been busy, Carter. You've been busy being a father and a husband."

Fuck.

I didn't say a single word because there was nothing I could say to help myself. It would only make it worse.

"Luca is a cute boy."

My hand immediately tightened into a fist at the mention of my son, the boy who was off-limits.

"Doing pretty well in school…except math. Doesn't take after you, I guess."

My pulse was so loud in my temples, I couldn't hear my own breathing. My eyes moved to the window, as if I expected twenty pairs of headlights to break down the gate at the front of my property.

"And your wife…exquisite as always. I would know…since I've fucked her so many times."

I closed my eyes and clenched my jaw, furious and heartbroken by the comment. I didn't care that Mia had been with other men—but I cared that she'd been fucked by another man against her will. I should have killed Egor when he least expected me. I should have put him in the ground so this conversation wouldn't be happening now.

"Carter, I'm disappointed in you. I had such a high opinion of you…but now I know you're just a thief."

I tried to think of a plan. The first thing I would do was contact my father and uncle. Griffin would be next. I would need to organize as many men as I could if I hoped to match Egor as an opponent. I wasn't letting this man hurt my family—not again.

"Have you nothing to say?"

I couldn't hold my silence forever. "I'm willing to settle this like a man."

"Really?" he asked. "Good. I was hoping you would say that. If you're an honorable man, you will return the stolen good—along with the boy."

Over my dead body. "I'll do you one better. I'll buy her from you."

"How can you buy something from me when I don't have it?" he countered. "And we both know that's not what I want."

"A hundred million," I offered. "And we're even."

"Oh, we'll never be even, Carter. I expect you to

pay a fee for your actions—in addition to giving her back to me."

Never. "Egor, that's not gonna happen. You know that." I would rather die than let him take my wife and son. I would take a bullet in the heart to spare them. "I say we find another compromise."

"Carter…be very careful."

A stretch of tense silence ensued. His threat was audible, but I had no idea what it meant.

"This is your last chance. Give Mia back to me, along with her son. Or there will be consequences you can't afford to suffer. Trust me on that…"

The fact that he wouldn't tell me specifically what it was terrified me, but there was nothing more terrifying than giving up my family. "I don't want to fight you, Egor. I want to settle this. But I'm not going to—"

"That is your final decision?"

Fuck.

"Carter?"

"Yes…it's my final decision."

"I figured it would be. Alright, then. Let me tell you a little story…"

I wished I had another phone to call my father and relay all this to him.

"I'm sitting in the back seat of a black car. I'm in Florence. There's this beautiful woman walking down the street, brown hair, green eyes…gorgeous figure."

No.

"If you won't give me Mia, then I'll take something else—your sister."

"You fucking piece of—"

"Goodbye, Carter. When I fuck her, I'll think of you." Click.

I dropped the phone as I launched to my feet. I snatched it back off the desk and pulled up my father's number. My hands were shaking so much that I nearly dropped it again. I finally got the phone to start ringing and placed it against my ear. "Pick up!"

It rang twice before my father answered. "Son—"

"Egor is going after Carmen right now. He's in Florence. She's walking. He sees her. We've got to do something." Words tumbled out of my mouth like vomit. I probably didn't make any sense over the phone.

But my father got it. "I'm leaving now. Stand outside your front gate. Crow and I will pick you up on the way."

"Hurry."

Click.

20

CARMEN

BOSCO HAD to work that night at the casino.

Apparently, Ronan needed the night off.

Just one night without him was torture. I couldn't wait until the casino was officially in the past and he wouldn't be gone during the night anymore. No more cigar smoke, tits, and Ruby.

It would be a quiet life for the two of us.

And I loved the home he'd bought. I wanted to see the inside of it, but I didn't want to get ahead of ourselves. My father still didn't like him yet.

I'd been skipping work a lot lately, so I decided to get a ride down there to do some bookkeeping. The guys dropped me off, and I looked through my paperwork in the back. I tallied up all my expenses for tax purposes, and a few hours later, I left.

I decided to pick up a pizza from my favorite local place a few blocks away, and it seemed pointless to call for the car, so I walked the few blocks and turned left. I pulled out my phone and called the order in, getting a Margherita pizza with extra cheese.

I liked extra cheese.

I got a call from one of Bosco's men when I was done.

"Hello, Carmen," he said in a professional tone. "Are you still in the shop?"

I must have slipped out in the two seconds they weren't watching.

"The lights are out."

"I walked a few blocks over to pick up a pizza. You can meet me there if you want."

There was so much panic in his silence. "We'll be right there. Bosco gave us very specific orders not to let you walk around at night alone."

"Well, I'm two blocks away. I'm sure I'll be fine." I hung up then kept walking. I turned right again and made my way up the quiet street. There was no traffic except a black car that passed in the opposite direction. The windows were completely blacked out. It made a U-turn and then came up behind me.

I knew it was Bosco's men, so I didn't look over my shoulder.

I could see the sign to the pizza place jutting out from the building. It had a picture of a cheesy slice along with the name of the restaurant. I knew his men would pick up anything I asked for, but it seemed ridiculous to order someone to do something that I could do myself. Besides, it was nice to walk.

The car stopped behind me, and all the doors opened.

I rolled my eyes, unable to believe they were really going to follow me on foot. "I'll be right back, boys. I can make it the rest of the way."

"Wow, you've got spunk." A distinct Russian accent sounded behind me, sinister, cold, and terrifying.

I stopped in my tracks, knowing this wasn't one of Bosco's men. I turned around, the panic already rising in my blood. My heart thumped against my rib cage, and I tried to think of something to do next. Bosco's men were just around the corner, so there was nothing to be scared of yet.

My eyes met a pair of blue ones. They were bright, almost the color of the sky on a summer day, not deep the way Bosco's were. With a few scars on his face and a lanky body, he seemed like the kind of criminal who had other men do his dirty work.

That didn't make him any less scary.

I chose to be brave, knowing Bosco's men would save me like they had in the past. "I was just about to get a pizza. Want a slice?"

He wore a navy blue suit, his hands in his pockets. Three men stood behind him, all carrying rifles that were pointed to the ground. He slowly walked toward me, smiling with crooked teeth. "I'm liking you more and more."

The sound of several gunshots erupted in the distance. The noises ricocheted off the buildings, audible from a few blocks over. They were so loud, my eardrums stung. My body jolted, and the terror gripped me.

"The men are taken care of," one of the guys reported to the Russian.

Jesus Christ, I was in trouble.

Another black car emerged from the other side of the street. It pulled up alongside the first. Four more men got out.

If Bosco's men were dead, then there was no way for the others to know I was in danger. There was no way for Bosco to know I was in danger. I would be taken by this man, and Bosco may never find me.

Enough jokes about pizza.

The Russian studied me as he slowly crept up to me. "A woman like you is smart to keep bodyguards. Too bad they weren't good at their jobs."

I had no idea who this man was. He obviously didn't know those men worked for Bosco, so why was he after me? Did it have something to do with my family? Or Griffin? "Those men belong to Bosco Roth. I also belong to Bosco Roth. So you should consider your next actions carefully."

That actually stopped him in his tracks, his smile weakening at the threat I'd just unleashed. He clearly hadn't taken the time to do his research before he approached me, because this was news to him.

"He's a possessive man. You should leave while you still can."

He recovered from the surprise and kept moving forward, approaching me with a cruel look in his eyes.

I didn't take a step back, knowing there was nowhere for me to go.

When he was right in front of me, he lifted the back of his hand to my face and felt my cheek with the backs of his fingers. "So soft…so flawless."

His breath smelled like cigarettes, and his slimy hands were ice-cold. He smelled like the back of a taxi, soaked with the scent of so many things it smelled like the odor from a skunk. With disgusting features and an even more disgusting presence, a grosser man had never touched me.

I pushed his hand away. "Don't touch me——"

He backhanded me hard, so hard I flew into the cold concrete. "I'm going to enjoy doing that to you—over and over."

It was the second time a man had hit me—and I was getting really sick of it. I didn't stay on the ground long because I refused to bend to a man. I refused to accept defeat. I pushed my way up again and silently threatened him with my gaze. My cheek was pulsing with inflammation, and I knew my cheek would be red for days. "You'll die for that."

He smiled, like that was the response he was hoping for. "You're just like Mia. I was hoping you would be."

Mia. The only terrible man who would know Mia

258   PENELOPE SKY

would have to be… It only took me a few seconds to figure out who he was. He was the man who'd raped and tortured my sister-in-law, the one who took away her ability to have children.

No way in hell was I gonna let him do that to me.

"You motherfucker." Just as my father taught me, I gave him a right hook that happened so fast he didn't see it coming. It wasn't packed with as much momentum because I didn't have as much time to draw back, but my fist landed where it belonged.

He turned with the hit and grabbed at his face.

All the men aimed their weapons at me.

"You're going to regret that, sweetheart." He slowly turned back to me, his eye already swelling.

"No. I don't think so." I threw my leg up to kick him in the balls.

He grabbed my leg and threw me on the ground.

My back hit the concrete and my body screamed in pain, but the adrenaline kept me on my guard.

"I'm gonna break your leg just to teach you a lesson." He snatched my ankle and dragged me toward him.

Shit, he was serious. "Get off me!" I kicked as hard as I could, refusing to be crippled so he could beat me even more. How did Mia survive years of this if I couldn't last even a few minutes?

"Help me," he ordered his men. "I'm breaking it right at the knee."

"You psycho!" I threw my whole body into it, fighting with everything I had.

Two men came and pinned me to the concrete so I couldn't move at all.

"Mia said the same thing." He grinned then positioned my leg. He looked down at me with a sneer. "On the count of three."

Oh my fucking god.

I tensed for the pain and prepared not to show it.

I'd never been so scared in my life.

Bosco, where the fuck are you?

"One." He grinned wider, seeing the sweat form on my forehead. "Two…"

Jesus Christ.

Gunshots rang out.

The two men holding me were down.

"Oh, thank god!" Egor looked up to see the commotion, so I yanked my leg back then kicked him hard in the chest.

He flew back.

"Take that, cunt!"

Cars filled the block, and the men fired at each other.

Egor scrambled to his feet to sprint away.

"Little bitch, you're mine." I lunged at him and got him by the ankle, bringing him to the ground. "How about I break your leg, huh?"

He turned around and struck me in the face.

I was immune to pain now. There was too much adrenaline, too much hostility. He did something unforgivable to my family, and I wasn't letting him get away. "I'm gonna kill you for what you did to my sister." I'd never killed anyone in my life, but I had no hesitation to do it now. I got on top of him and whaled on him, slamming my fists into his face. "Motherfucker!" I kept hitting him.

He shoved me off, his face bloody. Then he kicked me back, getting himself free.

Suddenly, all the sound died away. The gunshots were over because one side of the battle was dead.

Heavy footsteps approached. "Take her away." Bosco's deep voice was different than usual, full of rage he'd never expressed around me before. He didn't care about me at all. He had eyes only for the man who'd made the mistake of crossing me.

Two of Bosco's men came and helped me to my feet.

"Bosco, I—"

Bosco held up his hand and silenced me—without even looking at me. "Carmen, you aren't going to want to see this. Go to the car."

I didn't say another word, knowing the man I loved wasn't available right now.

His men guided me to the sidewalk and then opened the back door. I hesitated before I got inside.

Bosco stood over Egor and didn't say a word until I was out of harm's way for good.

The battery to the car was still on, so I cracked the

window when no one was watching, wanting to hear everything that was about to happen.

Egor spat blood out of his mouth before he looked up at Bosco.

Bosco stared at him with the same rage as before, his body so still it didn't seem like he was really alive. He looked like a statue, a spirit that had come to bring Egor into hell. "You killed my men. You touched my woman. You know what your punishment will be."

Egor didn't show any fear even though there was no possibility he wasn't scared.

"I will burn your men alive for what they did to mine."

I looked to the left and saw the men handcuffed in a group, most of them bleeding from their wounds. The streets were silent because no one was stupid enough to go outside right now. The police steered clear. I shouldn't feel bad for what the men were about to go through, but I did. Being burned alive seemed harsh.

Bosco wore a black suit with a black tie, sleek and stylish in contrast to what everyone else was wearing. With broad shoulders and wrath in his jawline, he looked like the executioner he always told me he was. "And I will slit your throat right here for what you did to my woman. I will watch the light leave your eyes, and I will fill the sewers with your blood."

My god, Bosco wasn't kidding.

"Any last words?" Bosco extended his hand to one of his men, silently asking for a blade.

One of them unsheathed a knife from his own belt and placed it in Bosco's palm.

Bosco gripped it and held it at his side, his fingers exploring the grip.

I opened the car door and got out. "He's the one who tortured Mia." I wanted Bosco to know that this man deserved the highest amount of suffering, that he didn't even deserve last words. Every man deserved one last wish—but not this guy.

Bosco's men motioned me to get back in the car.

Bosco didn't take his eyes off his captive, as if he didn't acknowledge what I'd said. "You raped and tortured an innocent woman for three years—and took her away from her son." He gripped the blade even harder, making his knuckles turn white.

I knew the part about Luca bothered him the most since he'd lost his own mother.

Egor stared at him but didn't confirm it. "You are—"

Bosco moved in a flash, yanking him by the hair and dragging him across the sidewalk.

Egor grunted and tried to swat his hands away.

When Bosco had him right next to the sewer, he brought his knife to Egor's throat and did the job, making Egor look into the sewer as he did it. "Your blood isn't even good enough for shit." He released his hair and let him fall forward, the blood dripping everywhere.

Egor made choking sounds until he bled out and died.

I watched the whole thing, wanting to see this man dead.

Bosco stared at him even when it was certain Egor was dead. "Burn his men alive," he ordered, holding out the bloody knife for someone to take. "And leave his body here. Tell the police not to move it until it starts to rot."

Just when I thought this was all over, more cars pulled up.

The men raised their weapons and prepared to fire.

I recognized the man who rose from behind the driver's door. It was my father.

"Lower your weapons," Bosco commanded his men with a subtle wave of his hand.

My father didn't care about Egor or Bosco. "Where is she?"

Carter got out of the passenger seat. Uncle Crow was with them too. They were all armed with artillery too. They must have known Egor was coming to get me, but since they had to drive from Tuscany, it took them much longer to get here.

I got out of the car. "Father, I'm okay."

His eyes settled on me, and a wave of relief flashed across his face—and then the tears emerged. "Sweetheart." He ran to me and wrapped his arms around me, his body acting as a cocoon to keep me safe. He cupped the back of my head and pressed his face against my forehead.

I felt his tears drip onto my face.

"My little girl…" He squeezed me harder and wept, not caring about the dozens of men standing around watching. He didn't care about Bosco. He didn't care about crying in front of his brother. "The whole drive here… I couldn't…" He couldn't get the words out, overcome with emotion. He was the strongest man I'd ever known, and not once in my life had I see him cry.

I cried too. "I'm okay…"

He kissed my forehead three times, his hands cupping my face. "I know. That's why I can't stop crying." He pulled away and allowed me to see the tears that reflected in his eyes. "Because I'm so damn grateful you're okay. It's hard enough to know what Mia went through…but not my girl too."

Watching him cry made me cry harder. "I'm right here… I'm not going anywhere. I'm safe. Egor's gone…"

"I know." He closed his eyes for a second and took a deep breath, forcing himself to bottle up his emotion. "Your face is red. Do you need to see a doctor?"

"No. I hurt him way more than he hurt me."

A painful smile moved onto his lips. "Attagirl." He cupped my cheeks and kissed me on the forehead. "I love you so much, Carmen. I can't even begin to describe…"

"I know you do… I love you too."

He looked at me again and wiped his tears on the sleeve of his jacket. He cleaned up the best he could before he turned back to Bosco and everyone else. He obviously wasn't ashamed of his tears.

Bosco met his gaze then nodded to Egor's body. "I took care of it."

Carter was standing over the corpse. He stared without blinking, and then without preamble, he spat on him.

Crow stayed in the back, his gun in his holster because there was no more fighting to do.

Bosco looked just as pissed off as before. "This is the man who hurt Mia. Why is he after my woman?" He didn't seem to care how he referred to me in front of my family. He was still in the fog of war, acting savage and barbaric. He'd acted this way when he fought The Butcher in the ring. There was no reasoning with him when he got like this.

Carter pulled his gaze away from Egor. "He found out that I had Mia. He called me and said he wanted her back. When I refused, he said he would take my sister instead. He didn't tell me that he was right behind her until a second before he hung up."

Bosco stared at Carter for a few seconds before he turned his gaze back on my father. He stared at him like he hated him as much as Egor. There was nothing but bloodshed in his eyes, like killing Egor once wasn't enough. "You never would have made it on time."

My father said nothing, but he held Bosco's gaze.

Bosco stepped closer to him. "You wouldn't have fucking made it on time." He slammed his hand into his own chest. "I did. I'm here. I protect her. I slit his goddamn throat, and I would do it again in a heartbeat. She's not in danger because of me—but because of you." He pointed right at my father's chest.

My father had just broken down right in front of me. I couldn't let him be yelled at right now. "Bosco, that's enough." I walked up to him and gently guided him back.

Bosco wouldn't look at me. "This was your fault. You fucked up—"

"Enough." I yanked on his arm. "I said, enough."

Bosco kept staring at my father, but he didn't disobey me.

My father spoke. "Carmen, he's right. He's absolutely right." He came closer to Bosco, all his hostility and anger gone. Now there was just a broken man left behind, a man crushed by what had just happened to his daughter. The thought of losing me was enough to humble him into silence. "I wouldn't have made it quickly enough. I wouldn't have had enough men. I wouldn't have saved my daughter…if it weren't for you." He took a deep breath, stilling the tears that wanted to emerge in his eyes again. "I owe you my life. I owe you everything. And…you've proven that you're right. And I'm wrong."

Bosco's face finally softened, his furor slowly disappearing like smoke from a dying fire.

"You can protect my daughter. I feel better knowing that she has you, that you can save her better than I ever could. I would have hunted Egor down and never stopped until I found him…but she would have already been captured, and that would have been enough to haunt me." He extended his hand. "Thank you, Bosco. I mean that…"

I waited for Bosco to reciprocate, hoping he wasn't too high on blood lust to be reasonable.

But he wasn't. He shook my father's hand. "You're welcome, sir."

My father nodded before he dropped his hand. "A good man wouldn't have been able to stop that from happening…"

"No, he wouldn't," Bosco said in agreement. "A Barsetti woman doesn't need a good man. She needs a powerful man, the kind of man who can move mountains and planets. That's me."

Father nodded again. "I think you're right." He stepped away and walked to Carter, placing his hand on his shoulder as they both stared at Egor's body. My father spat on him too.

Bosco turned to me, his eyes smoldering the second he looked at the puffiness of my cheek.

"It doesn't hurt," I said. "It felt so good to punch him in the face. It felt so good to watch him die. I'm glad all of this happened…because he didn't deserve to take another breath. It's a gift you've given to my family. Thank you."

"I didn't do it for them. I did it for you."

"I know…"

He moved into me and cupped my cheeks, his hands soft and comforting against my skin. He kissed the corner of my eye where the bruising started. "I'm glad you're okay. I'm sorry I didn't get here quicker."

"You were right on time."

He pulled away and gave me a sad look. "I want to be more affectionate with you." He pulled his hands away. "But I'm just so angry right now." He lowered his hands to his sides again. "I need some time." He stepped back, like he was afraid to touch me.

I remembered the way he was after he killed The Butcher. It took him the rest of the next day to get back to normal. There was still so much carnal rage in his veins. He wasn't the same. He turned into an animal. "I understand, babe." I touched his shoulder gently before I walked to my uncle.

He still stood back, giving my father and brother a moment alone with Egor's corpse. He wrapped his arm around my shoulders and held me like I was his daughter. "When I got Vanessa back in Morocco, I cried. She's a grown woman, but she'll always be my little girl. I remember the first time I held her. Just the thought of something terrible hurting something so beautiful…is enough to break the strongest man. Your father loves you the same way. And I love you too." He kissed my temple.

"I know, Uncle Crow. I love you too."

"I like Bosco."

"You do?" I asked.

"He's rough around the edges, but any man who's experienced real life is bound to be that way. He reminds me of Griffin—which is a great compliment."

"It is."

"I think your father has changed his mind about him."

"Yeah, I think so too. As he should…"

He patted my back gently. "Cut him some slack. He just loves you."

"I've never held a grudge against him for it. I know his feelings came from a good place."

"They always do." He lowered his arm. "Something good came out of this. Now we never have to worry about that piece of shit again. Mia deserved real justice —now she has it."

"Carter does too." I knew Egor must still haunt Carter since he loved Mia so much.

"Yeah. Now they both have some peace." His eyes moved to Bosco, who stood off to the side alone. His hands rested in his pockets as he stared at Egor's body. His men moved in the background and departed with the prisoners they took. They slowly cleaned up the screen and sprayed the blood off the pavement. "He doesn't look happy."

"He's just…still angry. He wishes he could kill Egor again. Once isn't enough."

Crow nodded. "I know how that is…"

My father and Carter came back, my father's hand on Carter's shoulder. "I guess we'll head home. The wives are all upset right now."

"I told Pearl everyone is okay," Uncle Crow said. "I'm sure she told the others."

My brother hugged me. "I'm so sorry, Carmen. This is all my—"

"I'm glad it happened. I'm glad Bosco killed him. I'm glad that our family can have some real peace. Mia deserves this justice. I'd gladly get hit in the face again for that joy. It was totally worth it."

Carter pulled away and gave me a slight smile. "Well, I wish you didn't have to get hit in the face…but I'm glad he's dead too. Really glad. It's like…a huge weight off my chest. I would still think about him, anxious that he would figure it out and swarm my house. But now, I never have to worry about it again."

"None of us do."

Carter glanced at Bosco before he looked at me again. "He's alright in my book, in case you were wondering."

"I wasn't," I teased.

He smiled. "Maybe he and I can hang out. Get to know each other."

"He would love that. All he has is his brother. I know he would love it if we could all make him feel like family. He lost his mom a few years ago, and he says he hasn't been himself ever since."

"Until he met you," Carter said. "At least, that's what my guess is."

———

It wasn't until a few hours later when we returned to the penthouse.

Wordlessly, Bosco shed his clothes and got into the shower.

I watched him from the doorway, watched him just stand there as the warm water dripped down his muscular frame. The warm water must have soothed him because he didn't seem to care about shampooing his hair or rubbing soap across his body.

I took off my clothes and joined him even though he asked for his space. I came up behind him and rested my forehead against his back, my hands holding on to his triceps. I let the warm water cleanse me, wipe away the dirt under my fingernails. I was frozen from hitting the cold concrete so many times, and I didn't realize how numb I was until I started to thaw.

He didn't react to my touch or ask me to leave.

After a few minutes passed, he turned around and lifted my chin so I would look him in the eye. There was still a hint of violence in his eyes, but the softness was beginning to return. "I wouldn't be able to go on if I lost you."

My fingers wrapped around his wrist. "I know."

"I don't judge your father for crying, because I would have cried too."

"I know."

He kissed my forehead then my lips. "I know you're a tough woman who can handle herself pretty well. I know you're strong enough to not let this hurt you, to overcome it, to not be afraid of what could have been. That helps me too…helps me let it go."

"Honestly, I'm happy all of this happened. If given the choice, I would have done it again. I knew you were coming for me. I just had to be a little more patient this time."

"I will always come for you. Bullets and knives can't stop me."

"I know. And that's why my father shook your hand and admitted he was wrong. In case you haven't noticed…he never admits he's wrong."

Finally, a ghost of a smile appeared on his lips. "Yeah…I noticed."

I pressed my face to his chest and kissed the muscles over his heart. "So, should I cancel the lease on my apartment? It sucks paying for a place I don't even use."

His hand rubbed the back of my neck. "You should have done that a long time ago."

"I'll pay you what I normally pay in rent."

He gave me such a terrifying look.

"Or not…"

He dropped his outrage and rubbed my neck again.

The last thing I wanted to do was piss him off after

he'd just killed someone a few hours ago. "So, I'm gonna move in, then? Officially?"

"Please."

"I'd love to. This place has felt like home since the first time I visited."

"Because it is home—your home." He kissed me again, loving my lips delicately.

I smiled as I felt his embrace. "So…you want to fuck me savagely like last time?"

He smiled, but his eyes turned even more intense than before. "Yes."

21

BOSCO

I WALKED across the floor of the casino, silently saying goodbye to the building that had housed all my dreams and aspirations. From a young age, I'd always been ambitious, always wanted a better life for my family.

I accomplished it.

Not only was I wealthy, but I had power.

I'd been powerless to help my mother when I was young. She'd had to beg for jobs to make ends meet, and one time when she couldn't, we were kicked out of our apartment. I never wanted her to feel powerless like that ever again. I didn't want to feel powerless either.

But now I was walking away from all of it.

Without a hint of bitterness.

I looked at the men playing at the tables, holding their hands of cards while cigars stuck out of their mouths. The women danced overhead, and topless waitresses couldn't get drinks served quick enough.

I remembered when this room was empty. The day I bought it, it was a rathole.

Now it was an empire.

"Hey, Bosco." Ruby's sexy voice emerged from my right. She stepped from the shadows of one of the power tables, walking through the cloud of smoke that made the room hazy. "Where's your lady friend?"

I kept walking. "Home."

"She's feisty, isn't she?" She smoked a cigar as she walked, wearing a red gown with a sweetheart neckline.

"I'm gonna cut to the chase, Ruby." I stepped forward and faced her, not attracted to her curves anymore. "I'm marrying her. This—" I pointed between the two of us "—is never gonna happen again. She's the woman getting my money. Stop wasting your time and find someone else. I'm selling the casino, so I'm probably not interesting to you anymore."

She hid her disappointment at my speech. "Who are you selling it to?"

"Ronan, obviously."

"Oh…so now he has the moneybags."

He always had the moneybags since we split the profits. But it didn't matter. "He's all yours." I walked away from her, hoping that was the last time I would ever see her again.

I took the elevator to the office to meet Ronan. It was strange to see him sitting behind my desk. He'd changed a few things in the room—but kept the picture of the three of us. I sat in the leather chair where Carmen and I had once slept.

Ronan eyed me. "You're sure?"

I nodded. "Yes."

"This must be hard for you. I can tell you don't like me sitting behind your desk."

"*Your* desk," I corrected. "And no, I don't." I grinned. "I'll get used to it." I had a lot more to look forward to.

"So…marriage…babies… You still want that?"

I tapped my fingers against the armchair. "Yes, eventually. But right now, I'm happy with the way things are. Carmen is a lot younger than me, so there's no rush."

"I don't know…she's twenty-five. She probably wants to get started soon."

"Well, she knows my dick is available at her command, so I'm ready whenever she is."

He chuckled. "Ain't that truth. Well, I'm gonna miss seeing you around here. You won't come by for a game or two?"

"No. I told her father I wouldn't be associated with this place anymore. My goal is to disappear."

"I hope that means you won't be disappearing from my life too…" It seemed like a joke, but I knew there was a hint of seriousness to it.

"Never. We'll have you over for dinner once a week."

He grinned. "Now, I'm down with that."

"Carmen really likes you. She wants you around as much as I do."

"That woman is lovely. You fucked around for so long, but your dick knew when it found the right one."

I placed my hand over my heart, even though it was cheesy. "No. My heart did."

Ronan laughed, but he didn't tease me. "I'm happy for you. I hope I find that someday...not that I'm in a hurry."

"When the time comes, you'll know." I never walked anywhere, and the one time I did, I came across the most beautiful woman I'd ever seen—my future wife. "Let me know if you have any questions, even though I know you probably won't."

"I know this business like the back of my hand," he said. "But maybe I'll use it as an excuse to call."

I gave him a slight smile. "You don't need an excuse, man."

CARMEN'S APARTMENT WAS PACKED UP AND EMPTY. The lease was broken, and she'd redirected her mail to my penthouse.

She'd officially moved in.

I didn't ask her to marry me because there didn't seem to be a rush. The diamond was still in the box whenever she was ready to wear it. We were happy, so it didn't seem like I needed to hurry.

"Are you okay?" she asked when I walked in the door.

It was the last time my suit would smell like cigars. I would actually miss that. "I'm fine, Beautiful."

"I know it must be hard for you…" She pushed my jacket off my shoulders and rubbed my chest. "And that's okay if it is."

I stared at the beautiful woman who loved me, loved me for me and not my money. She didn't care about my power and was intimidated by it most of the time. This woman only wanted me. I knew how lucky I was to have her, that not all men could have such an extraordinary woman. "It was a little hard when I left the office. But when I remembered what I was coming home to, it wasn't so bad." My hands gripped her hips, and I held her against my chest, treasuring the petite woman I would love the rest of my life. She was the only woman I would fuck, the only woman I'd ever made love to. The thought wasn't scary at all.

Her eyes softened in the most adorable way. She cupped my cheek and placed a kiss on my lips. "I love you, babe."

I loved that nickname. It was a pussy name, but I liked it anyway. I liked the affection, the way she called me that by accident the first time she said it. It was the first time I knew she loved me, the first time I under-stood how possessive she was of me. "I love you too, Beautiful." My hand slid under the fall of her hair as I enjoyed her lips. "I'll love you for the rest of my life."

EPILOGUE

CARMEN

ONCE I SAT in the chair at the dining table, I couldn't get up again. "Oh my god, I'm so fat, I can't even move." I placed my hand on my stomach and groaned as my knees and back ached. I was carrying a litter, and my body couldn't handle the twin boys growing inside me.

"If I can give birth to Crow junior, then you can do this," Vanessa said across the table from me, her pregnant belly only three months along.

Griffin was beside her, holding their son in his arms. Young Crow was asleep, passed out after a busy day of swimming in the sun.

"My back killed me too," my mother said. "With both of you. It sucks, but it's so worth it in the end."

"You told me that last time," I said sarcastically. "And that's debatable."

My father came out of the kitchen holding Emily by

the hand, my two-year-old daughter who liked to rock a side ponytail. He tickled her tummy, making her giggle. "I gave her some ice cream, Carmen."

"I told you she can't have dessert before dinner." I was a lot more irritable than I used to be since my belly was getting so big. Now anything pissed me off.

"Not my problem," Father said. "I love being a grandparent."

"Wait," I said. "You never let us get away with stuff like that when we were little."

Father shrugged. "I like being a grandpa more than a father. It's more fun." He took Emily into the other room to play with Luca, even though he was a lot older than she was.

"Babe." I sat back and rubbed my stomach.

Bosco came out of the kitchen. He was cooking with my brother and uncle, trying to whip up a dinner that could feed nearly twenty people. "Beautiful, are you doing alright?" He kneeled down and placed his left hand on my stomach, his black wedding ring visible.

"I think I need some ice cream," I blurted.

Mom laughed. "He's in the middle of making dinner, and you're going to ask him for ice cream?"

"Father just gave my daughter some, so now I want some," I demanded. "I've got two babies in here."

Bosco kissed my stomach, amused by my request, not annoyed. "Coming right up, Beautiful."

"Way ahead of you." Ronan came up behind him with a bowl of vanilla ice cream, hot fudge, and sprinkles. "I know how she likes it." He set the bowl in front of me with a spoon. "Anything else?"

"You're my favorite brother," I said, partially joking and partially not.

Carter's voice sounded from the kitchen. "I heard that."

I rolled my eyes.

Bosco rose to his feet then rubbed the back of my neck. "Dinner is almost ready."

"Thanks for cooking," I said. "My knees are killing me."

"I don't mind," he said. "Just relax. I've got it." He smiled then turned away.

"You're so nice to my daughter, Bosco," my mother said. "Even when she doesn't deserve it."

He turned back around and looked at me. "She's giving me twins. She can ask for whatever she wants." He walked back into the kitchen to help my brother and uncle.

The house was packed with all our family members. We'd invited them over for another Sunday dinner, and while I loved having everyone here, I wished I wasn't so pregnant. I was excited to have another baby, but I'd never expected to have twins.

"And you're going to do this two more times," Aunt Pearl said. "So, pace yourself."

"Uh, no," I said. "Just one more time. That makes four babies."

"But that's only three pregnancies," Mom said. "That's cheating."

I grabbed my bowl of ice cream and started to eat. "Do you want me to have more kids or something? Mia and Carter have two kids, and we're gonna have four. That's six grandkids. That's so many Christmas presents."

Mom shrugged. "The more kids, the better. That's just my opinion."

"True." Aunt Pearl picked up Crow Jr. from Griffin. "Grandkids really are the best."

I finished my bowl of ice cream in less than a minute and then rubbed my stomach again. The frozen treat helped me cool off since it was the middle of summer in Tuscany. The air cranked, but there were so many people in the house, it couldn't be controlled.

Bosco came back into the room and placed a glass of ice water in front of me. "You need anything else?"

"I didn't ask for this."

"Yeah, but I noticed you didn't have anything." Bosco had turned into the most attentive husband and caring father I'd ever seen. It didn't seem like it was possible years ago, but he fit the role perfectly, like that's what he was meant to be.

"Aww…you're so sweet." My hormones were all over the place, so just a glass of water was touching to me. "Thank you. You're so good to me." I grabbed his hand and squeezed it. "There's no one else in the world I would give birth to twins for besides you."

He chuckled then kneeled in front of me again. "And there's no other woman I would give up everything to raise a family with…and be the happiest man in the world because of it." He held my gaze with sincerity in his eyes, not caring that my family was there watching the entire thing.

Again, he touched my emotions. "Bosco…"

He brought my hand to his mouth and kissed it. "I mean it."

"I know you do."

He placed my hand over his heart. "It beats for you." He rose to his feet again and kissed me on the forehead before he walked back into the kitchen.

When I turned back to my family, they were all staring at me—grinning.

Even Griffin was.

"That man's got it bad for you—still," Mom said. "Even when you're seven months pregnant."

"I know," I said quietly. "I'm very lucky. The luckiest woman in the world."

AFTERWORD

Thank you so much for taking this journey with me. I truly love the Barsettis and am grateful you indulged me as I got to know each of them so much better.

If you haven't read the Scotch series, you might check out The Scotch King…

Order Now